110659941

Acclaim for Daphne Kalotay's

Calamity and Other Stories

A *Poets & Writers Magazine* Notable Book of the Year
A *Boston Herald* Editors' Choice Selection

"Daphne Kalotay's stories . . . are old-fashioned in the best
sense of the word, plainspoken and melancholy, about ordinary people struggling with the trials of ordinary life. Few writers I know speak . . . with such clear-eyed compassion, such
quiet humor and grace."

—Jhumpa Lahiri, Pulitzer Prize—winning
author of *Interpreter of Maladies* and *The Namesake*

"These stories, simply told and insightful, make for entertain-
ing reading."   —*The Sunday Oklahoman*

"Daphne Kalotay pursues the ongoing arc of her characters' lives
in subtle, languid, sometimes oblique ways."

—*The Improper Bostonian*

"Kalotay's stories offer an intimate glimpse at . . . the absurdities
and delights of an ordinary life."   —*The Virginian-Pilot*

Daphne Kalotay

Calamity
and Other Stories

Born and raised in New Jersey, Daphne Kalotay is a
graduate of Vassar College and of Boston University,
where she received an MA in creative writing and a
Ph.D. in literature. Her short stories have appeared
in various literary journals and magazines, and she
has taught literature and writing at Middlebury College and Boston University. She lives in Brookline,
Massachusetts.

Daphne
Kalotay

Anchor Books
A Division of Random House, Inc.
New York

Calamity

and

Other

Stories

FIRST ANCHOR BOOKS EDITION, MAY 2006

Copyright © 2005 by Daphne Kalotay

All rights reserved. Published in the United States by Anchor Books, a division
of Random House, Inc., New York, and in Canada by Random House of Canada
Limited, Toronto. Originally published in hardcover in the United States by
Doubleday, a division of Random House, Inc., New York, in 2005.

Anchor Books and colophon are registered trademarks of Random House, Inc.

This book is a work of fiction. Names, characters, businesses, organizations,
places, events, and incidents either are the product of the author's imagination
or are used fictitiously. Any resemblance to actual persons, living or dead,
events, or locales is entirely coincidental.

The Library of Congress has cataloged the Doubleday edition as follows:
Kalotay, Daphne.
Calamity and other stories / by Daphne Kalotay.—1st ed.
p. cm.
Contents: Serenade—A brand new you—All life's grandeur—Prom season—
Sunshine cleaners—The man from Allston Electric—Anniversary—Snapshots
—Difficult thoughts—Rehearsal dinner—Calamity—Wedding at Rockport.
1. United States—Social life and customs—Fiction. I. Title.
PS3611.A455C35 2004
813'.6—dc22
2004052701

Anchor ISBN-10: 1-4000-7848-2
Anchor ISBN-13: 978-1-4000-7848-6

Book design by Terry Karydes

www.anchorbooks.com

Printed in the United States of America
10 9 8 7 6 5 4 3 2 1

For

my parents

and

my sister

Acknowledgments

Enormous thanks and endless gratitude to: The Helene Wurlitzer Foundation, The Writers' Colony at Dairy Hollow, Eve Bridburg at grub street, inc., Leigh Feldman, Deb Futter, Leah Kalotay, Judy Layzer, Ron Nemec, Emily Newburger, Rishi Reddi, and Julie Rold.

Some of these stories have appeared elsewhere, in slightly altered form: "Serenade" in *The Missouri Review*, "All Life's Grandeur" in *Prairie Schooner*, "Sunshine Cleaners" in *Michigan Quarterly Review*, "The Man from Allston Electric" in *AGNI*, "Snapshots" in *The Literary Review*, "Calamity" in *AGNI*, "Prom Season" in *Good Housekeeping*.

Grateful acknowledgment is made for permission to reprint a portion of "I Knew a Woman," copyright © 1954 by Theodore Roethke, from *The Collected Poems of Theodore Roethke* by Theodore Roethke. Used by permission of Doubleday, a division of Random House, Inc.

Contents

Calamity
and
Other
Stories

Serenade

My mother believed that her entire life would have somehow been different had she been given piano lessons as a girl. She said this often, with a little sigh that made me feel I had better run through my scales one more time. She had grown up, as she often reminded me, "a sculptor's daughter," which I later learned to translate into "poor." I did not take the piano in our family room for granted. My parents found it at a garage sale, a big brown upright with the face of Ray Charles painted on the frontpiece. I always approached it reverently, with the impression that my piano lessons were going to somehow transform me.

In outright mimicry of my neighbor, Callie, I'd demanded that my piano instructor be Cole Curtin. He would appear at our doorstep chewing his thumbnail, invariably late, sheet music stuffed into a paper bag. Entering our house, he strained his neck to glimpse my mother chopping vegetables in the kitchen. In demonstrating a technique or correcting an error, he could play a ten-minute cadenza and then look surprised to find me sitting there beside him. After I'd struggled through my scales, his only reaction might be to say, "Your mother is extremely beautiful."

According to Callie, Mr. Curtin treated *her* mother no differently. Neither Callie nor I questioned such behavior. We were best friends, both of us ten years old, with a little brother each that we didn't much like. We lived next door to each other and owned identical yellow jumpers. It seemed appropriate that we have the same piano teacher, and that he be in love with both of our mothers.

My father might never have made the fuss about Mr. Curtin had he not been home from the office early one Thursday. In my worldview, fathers were either "at the office" or "on the porch." When mine came home, winter or summer, he retreated to the little screened-in space that nosed into our backyard. There he had installed a large rocking chair (it had been in the family, Russ and I were often reminded, for over one hundred years) next to a table full of wood for whittling. My mother explained this to us as "Daddy's downtime." Winters he would bundle up in a scarf and hat, wrap a wool blanket around himself, and nap there for an hour or so before creating some small object out of a piece of cedar.

Now it was July, and my father was home earlier than usual, whittling away on the porch. Peeking through the living room window, I saw Mr. Curtin approaching our front door, stopping at one of the planters to have a look at some petals or bugs. He was a soft-shouldered man, with thick dark brown hair, bushy eyebrows, and a droop to his eyes. Even though it was summer he wore the same fading corduroy pants as in winter, only now with five-and-dime flip-flops. His button-down shirt was tight on his shoulders, as if it had been purchased ten or so years earlier, before his body completed puberty's cycle. He was still young! Callie and I didn't know this. Mr. Curtin's tired eyes suggested a long, difficult past. His mumbled comments implied a history of lost opportunity and poor decisions: Women gone off with other men. Jobs lost unaccountably. Sheet music lent to students and never seen again.

He bore the slouch of someone perpetually waiting for a tow truck. And despite his thick build, he looked as though he needed to be fed; his skin was pale, and there was a neediness in the way he lingered by the kitchen door as I urged him into the family room.

"Hello, Melena," he said softly to my mother. She looked up from her cooking, and a shiny loop of dark hair swung across her face. "How are you, Cole?"

"Oh, you know," he said. "Things happen. I got fired from the ballet school." Days Mr. Curtin played accompaniment for dance classes.

"Why?" This was me.

"The teacher said I made her feel uncomfortable."

"I'm sorry to hear that," my mother said.

I asked, "Why? Why did you make her feel uncomfortable?"

"Quiet, Rhea. Don't be nosy."

"She said I kept looking at her. How could I not? She's there in those pink tights." Mr. Curtin sighed. "She has such a beautiful neck."

That was when my father came in and said, "Cole," with a little nod of his head, the way he did with everyone except children. "How's Rhea's progress?"

Mr. Curtin sighed again and said, "I suppose we'd better get started." We went to the family room, where the piano sat squarely against a clean white wall. Mr. Curtin listened to my scales and my études, and then I moved on to my pride and joy— real sheet music by a real composer. Other kids were playing "Four Jazzy Fingers and a Swingin' Thumb," but Mr. Curtin had given me and Callie the real thing—simple, elegant children's pieces by Bartók.

"Oh—ugh! Stop! You're murdering it!" he yelled when my fingers hammered at the keys. "It's a sin!" Then he mumbled something about how he didn't actually believe in sin, and after that he demonstrated how to play with appropriate sensitivity. His eyes closed and his head bowed, and beautiful music wafted into the kitchen, where my mother was sliding a casserole into the oven.

"You need to work on refinement, subtlety," Mr. Curtin told me. I didn't know what either of those words meant. "Here," he said. "Here's a beautiful little one, soft and sensual. Play this for your mother in the evening, when she's tired and wants to rest her eyes."

Leaving that night, he said, "Melena, your cooking smells wonderful," in a way that made me think he wanted to stay for

dinner. But the invitation he elicited was for the coming weekend.

"We're having people on Saturday," my mother said. "A sort of garden party. If you'd like to come."

"Yes," said Mr. Curtin.

"Starting five or so," my mother told him as she let him out the door. "See you then."

My father had left the porch to sit down at the dinner table. "I wish you hadn't done that," he said softly. "I wish you hadn't invited the piano teacher to our party."

"Why shouldn't I?" my mother asked, sounding truly surprised. "Rhea and Callie just love him, and I think it will be a treat for Cole, too. He doesn't have much money, Gordon. I'm not sure he eats."

"Melena, you know that Jerry Waslick is coming."

"What does your boss have to do with it?"

"I—maybe you don't think this way—" My father's voice sounded embarrassed. "You know I'm keeping my fingers crossed about the promotion. I'd like to be able to make a favorable impression on Saturday. I'm just not sure it's appropriate to invite a piano teacher who sleeps in his clothes and ogles girls in tights—"

"Not girls in tights," my mother said. "The teacher. She has a lovely neck." She laughed briefly. "He's perfectly cultured, Gordon. Why, he's more cultured than the both of us put together."

That was the last I heard of Mr. Curtin until the day of the party. "I'm wondering if we shouldn't look into a new piano teacher," my father said that morning as he frowned over a crossword. "Did you hear the language he used with Rhea the other night? 'Sensual.' Is that an appropriate word for a ten-year-old girl? No. Not for most people, if you get right down to it."

I was in the backyard tossing a ball with Russ, and so I had a fine view of both the porch and the kitchen window. "Most people don't have the intellectual side that we do—" I heard my mother say.

"Melena, please," my father said, sounding bored.

"Well, maybe you don't," said my mother coldly, "but I am the daughter of a sculptor. I know an artist when I see one, and I think that you greatly underestimate the value of a person like Cole."

"I have no doubt that he's as worthy as the next guy," my father said, squinting at the crossword. "It's that he's so . . . he's just a . . ." My father pulled a pencil from behind his ear and counted a line of crossword boxes. "Embarrassment," he declared.

The weather that evening was warm and breezy, and Callie and I had a good time running from the front lawn to the back in our matching jumpers, waiting for the first guest to arrive. But the first guests were Callie's parents, Tom and Helen. I was allowed to call them Tom and Helen because that was what Callie called them. Helen was blonde like Callie and winked whenever she was about to say something funny. She seemed always to be buying Callie Shetland sweaters and pink corduroy skirts and tiny pearl studs that I coveted almost painfully.

Tom, who was fifteen years older than Helen, often gave me

and Callie Bazooka bubble gum. This had prompted me to say to my mother one day, "Tom is so, so, so nice." My mother gave a reply that for years mystified me.

"*Too* nice," she said in a grave tone, with a chastising shake of her head. "Tom is too, too, too nice."

He and Helen showed up with spare martini shakers and a big punch bowl that Helen claimed had been in a box since 1966. "It was one of those impractical wedding gifts," she said. "As if now that you're married you're going to drink *punch.*"

"We probably thought it was terrific at the time," Tom said.

Helen said, "Dear, I doubt that whoever gave it to us is in hearing range. Admit it, you hate punch." And then she tossed back her head and yelled, "TOM HATES PUNCH!"

My mother giggled, and my father said, "In that case, how about some other drink. What can I get you?" Russ and Brian had already gone off dueling with their light sabers. Callie and I ran to the front yard to chant, "Tom hates punch!" as the guests began to arrive.

"Nice place you have here, Gordon," Jerry Waslick told my father. Both of them were wearing short-sleeved button-down shirts and leather boat shoes.

"Yeah, well, we've been thinking about building a pool," my father replied, though in fact this discussion had been dropped the previous summer. Too much maintenance, my father had insisted. But now he said, "We're still looking for the right people to do it."

Jerry Waslick began to tell my father all he knew about pools, while the two of them paced the backyard with their hands in their chinos. Remembering this now, it seems perfect that at just that moment, with my father listening to advice he never meant to implement, Mr. Curtin emerged from the quince bushes beside him. There was a trace of pollen on his pant cuffs, and he carried the same wrinkled paper bag he always used to transport sheet music. "I went to Callie's house by mistake," he explained as I ran up to him.

"Cole," my father said to him, with a nod and a frown.

Mr. Curtin, flustered, mumbled, "I came through the backyard." He looked around at the people on the lawn, and his gaze ended next to him, on Jerry Waslick, who whipped his right hand out of his pant pocket, offered it to Mr. Curtin, and said, "Jerry Waslick," in a way that indicated at once where my father had learned to nod his head.

"I'm Cole."

"Pleased to meet you," said Jerry Waslick.

"You are?"

Jerry Waslick seemed to think that this was the wittiest thing he had heard in a long time. While he laughed, my father said, "Here, why don't I get both of you a drink."

Helen had seen Mr. Curtin now and came over, saying, "Cole, how are you?"

"Fine. Well, no. Not really. Theo ran away." Theo was Mr. Curtin's Dalmatian, who seemed to always be in some sort of trouble. He had swallowed Mr. Curtin's one good pen, and broken the screen door. The last I'd heard, Theo had developed a fear of dust.

"I'm so sorry," Helen said. "When did it happen?"

"Two nights ago. I came home and he was all riled up, and

when I went through the front door he ran out, completely upset." Mr. Curtin hung his head for a moment. "I hadn't cleaned in a while, and I can't help but wonder . . ."

Jerry Waslick, who could not be blamed for thinking that Theo was human, appeared fascinated by the conversation. But my father led him away, saying, "Let me show you that sander I was telling you about."

Mr. Curtin shrugged his shoulders.

"I'd say you could use a drink," said Helen, who had already had a number of them herself. "Let me fix you something. Callie, I told you to stop eating all the pimentos."

"It's not pimento. It's red pepper." Not that it would have mattered. Callie had no qualms when it came to breaking rules, which was why it was always more fun to play at her house than at mine.

At this point old Millie Day, who had been invited only because she lived right across the street, saw us and said, "Todd? Are you Robert Fenwick's son? My, how you've grown!" But before Mr. Curtin could correct her, she shuffled off, saying, "I must tell Edna."

I remember the waning sun that evening, because it seemed to take forever to set. It gently stretched our guests' shadows across the lawn and turned orange in a showy way. With their hair lit from behind, everyone looked quite pleased with themselves. Callie and I ran around stealing cocktail cherries and olives and every once in a while listening in on a conversation.

"I don't know how I ended up here," I heard my mother saying to someone on the patio. She must have been drunk, because she had taken off her shoes; my mother usually complained of having to hide her long, callused toes. "I should be in a city," she said now, barefoot on a wooden bench, her hair curling in the humidity. "Or the country or something. I miss the company of artists." She took a sip of white wine and said, "You know, I was a sculptor's daughter."

I sat down on a stool nearby and nibbled celery. The woman to whom my mother was speaking was, it turned out, Edna LeBlanc, Millie Day's widowed elder sister. She lived with Millie and now appeared to be dozing. This did not faze my mother, who added, "But the school system's good. It's for the children, really. I want all the best for them. Cole! Well, now, when did you get here?"

"Oh, I don't know." Reaching into the wrinkled bag he still carried, Mr. Curtin took out two record albums. "I thought I'd bring some party music," he said, handing the records to my mother.

Her eyes opened wide, and she looked at the first record. "Glenn Gould playing Bach. Oh, Cole, how thoughtful of you."

"The other one is jazz, in case that's more the spirit of things," Mr. Curtin said, thrusting his hands into his pockets and looking down at his flip-flops.

My mother examined the other album and said, "Bill Evans. I'll put it on right away."

"I hope you like him," Cole called, as my mother went to the stereo on the porch. Meanwhile, Charlie Dibbs, my father's best friend, sat down on the bench where my mother had been. He looked at Mr. Curtin and said, "Gordon says you're the piano teacher."

Mr. Curtin nodded. "Hi. I'm Cole."

"Don't sound so apologetic about it." Charlie Dibbs took a sip of his sangria. He wore the best outfit of any of the men at the party: a short-sleeved pastel shirt, plaid shorts, pink, green and white argyle socks, and white tennis sneakers. My mother emerged, saying, "Charlie, have you met Cole? Cole is Rhea's piano teacher. He brought this record for us to listen to. Isn't it lovely?"

Mr. Curtin said, "Um, I think you've left it on the wrong speed."

My mother gave a laugh and said, "Oh my goodness! Of course! Too much wine already. Forgive me, Cole." She went off to attend to the record player and neglected to come back.

Charlie Dibbs and I remained on the patio with Mr. Curtin and Edna LeBlanc, listening to the jazz that floated over from the porch. "You play this stuff?" Charlie Dibbs asked.

"Not like this," Mr. Curtin said, and closed his eyes. I'd never seen anyone listen so attentively to a piece of music. He stayed like that for minutes, while Charlie Dibbs poked around at the fruit in his sangria. When Mr. Curtin remained silent, Charlie Dibbs began to look bored, and went so far as to try to rouse Edna LeBlanc with a tap on the elbow. She let out a hearty snore.

Finally Mr. Curtin opened his eyes and spoke. "If only life could be like this."

This statement appeared thoroughly unsatisfactory to Charlie Dibbs, who stretched his limbs, half stifled a belch, and said, "Whoa—that eggplant dip's already getting to me."

"Oh, good, you're still here." It was my mother, walking over, slightly wobbly. "I was thinking, Cole. I was thinking that maybe you could play for us later on."

Serenade

11

"Well, only if you think people would want to hear—"

"Oh, of course, of course," my mother told him, unaware that some wine was spilling from her glass. "Gordon. Gordon! Come help Cole roll the piano onto the porch."

"If it's a problem—" said Mr. Curtin.

"Not at all. Gordon! Come here and help Cole—"

"I heard you," my father called from the lawn. "In a minute, okay? Jerry wants to show me his Ford."

When my father returned, he made a big deal about pushing the piano, though it was on wheels, through the door from the family room onto the porch. I heard him telling Jerry Waslick, after Mr. Curtin had sat down to play, that used pianos often sounded better than brand new ones.

Mr. Curtin, meanwhile, closed his eyes and began to play Scarlatti. Callie, who liked to be part of a show, came and stood next to him as if she might be needed to turn pages. Public attention never flustered her, and with her honey-blond bob and perfectly straight bangs (the sort of thing my curls could never manage) she looked neat and efficient; you wouldn't have guessed that really she barely even practiced her scales. I stood tenuously behind her, to show that I too was a part of all this.

No one was really listening, but my mother and Helen acted as an audience, leaning back on the wicker loveseat directly across from the piano, their hair a tangle of blond streaks and dark curls. Helen rested her head on my mother's shoulder, while my mother whispered things that caused them both to giggle. They were holding hands. Helen whispered something back, and both of them burst out in a loud cackle just as Mr. Curtin settled into a pianissimo section of the sonata.

Perhaps it was that double laugh that caused Mr. Curtin to

look up. He saw that my mother had flung her head back, and laugh-tears were at the corners of her eyes. Helen, smiling, absently ran her finger along my mother's arched neck. My mother turned her head to Helen and, still laughing, placed her lips on Helen's mouth. That was when Mr. Curtin stopped playing. In the absence of music, Jerry Waslick's voice could be heard, saying, ". . . but we thought a canoe might be better." I turned to see my father standing with him, along with Charlie Dibbs and Tom. Only my father had looked up absently to see why the music had stopped. This all took place in a matter of seconds, and yet I can see so clearly, in stop-action, my father's gaze following that of Mr. Curtin, until it found my mother reclined there on the wicker furniture, her mouth already withdrawing from Helen's. For a brief moment my father looked as if he had bitten into a bad grape. But then his very posture changed. He let his hands drop to his sides in an awestruck way and regarded my mother and Helen with the same lonely, powerless look I had seen so many times on Mr. Curtin's face. Behind him, limp on the piano bench, Mr. Curtin, too, stared at them.

My mother and Helen weren't even kissing any more, just laughing in a tired way. If you had blinked you could have missed it. Callie did; she was leafing through my sheet music, making sure we were playing all the same pieces. My mother put her bare feet up on the wicker ottoman and took another sip of white wine. My father was returning to his old self now, and looked around with little jerks of his head to see if anyone had noticed the kiss. "Yeah, the Delaware Water Gap is nice," Jerry Waslick was saying, "but the mosquitoes will kill you."

Mr. Curtin was closing the piano now. He turned to me and Callie and said, "Nothing I could ever play could come near to the beauty of what we've just witnessed. That's the tragedy of my life."

Old Edna LeBlanc, who had woken, was making her way onto the porch with her sister. *"Tragedy,"* she said to Millie, as Mr. Curtin laid his head on the covered keyboard. "It's like I always say: these young ones don't know the meaning of the word."

A Brand New You

He sang in the shower—was singing, right now, in her shower.
Annie didn't remember him ever doing that before and couldn't
help feeling annoyed, not because she had anything against
singing in the shower, but because in Ben's case it seemed cal-
culated, to make her think how cute he was for being the sort of
person who sang in the shower. But Annie knew his ways all too
well, knew that if she weren't around to listen he probably
wouldn't even hum.

And yet she had married him. Fifteen years ago she had
married him, and eight years ago she had divorced him. And
now here he was singing in her shower, having just bedded her
for the first time in nine years.

She had found him that afternoon on Bleecker, where she

was killing time after her final class of the day, a summer seminar with a professor who bored her but who was supposed to be one of the greatest minds in modern philosophy. There she was, enjoying the June warmth and grime and people all around her, when she saw a man who looked like her ex-husband, with thick, wavy gray hair and matching gray eyes, and then saw, as he approached, that it indeed was him. Because she was feeling generous, she said, "Hey, you asshole!" and gave him a big kiss on the cheek.

She could tell that he was pleased by her looks. Sure enough, he said, "Annie, Jesus, you look amazing!" but then of course had to shake his head as though he hadn't thought it possible. Well, that was the most she could expect from him; it didn't matter any more. A week ago she had turned forty, and she felt better than she had in years. Her dark hair was newly permed, and she was wearing the stretchy rainbow-striped tube top that made the most of her broad bust. Her close-fitting Jordache jeans, a birthday present to herself, showed how strong her legs were now. She had quit smoking and even briefly considered quitting drinking, and her skin looked the better for it.

For a year now she had been heeding the advice of a health guru named Caleb Crantz, author of *A Brand New You* and *An Even Better Brand New You*. Together his books prescribed an entire way of living that was basically impossible to follow but a diverting challenge nonetheless. There were special foods to purchase and a special order in which to eat them, and there were suggested ways to move and to breathe. To protect the spine, for instance, Caleb Crantz advised against carrying anything. Anything. Not a shoulder bag, not a backpack, and even though Annie was now in graduate school and should have been carting wheelbarrows of books around campus like everyone else, she had made it through two semesters taking Crantz's advice to heart. He also proposed drinking nothing but filtered water, cooking only with organic ingredients, eating eight small meals—instead of three regular ones—a day, and walking instead of using any seated form of transportation. Annie's job at the cultural center was only three blocks away from her apartment in Brooklyn, but on class days she walked all the way to NYU, nibbling a bulgur-wheat scone at the prescribed hour and making sure to have a few small bills in her pocket in case she was mugged on the bridge. She arrived late for her classes and—because she wasn't supposed to carry anything—without books, notepads, or pens. Sometimes she borrowed pencils and paper to take notes that she then tossed into trash bins, since she couldn't carry them home. It didn't matter; she had a photographic memory. That was how she had graduated at the top of her class at Bryn Mawr.

Amazing, Annie had thought as she stood there across from Ben on the warm, littered sidewalk. Amazing that she could now be thinner and happier than she had been when she was thirty, stronger and more confident than when she was twenty-five. Perhaps because he was a full thirteen years older than Annie, Ben had always treated her with a certain authoritative judgment, and even as he stood there on Bleecker Street, he did that thing he always did, letting his eyes quickly scan her, head to toe, giving an approving nod. Eight years ago she would have found it annoying, offensive even, but now that she no longer had to admit to the public that he was hers, it was simply flattering. Annie could be a liberated woman and still accept compliments from an asshole like Ben. It had taken her—and so many women—all of the 1970s to figure that out.

Ben looked basically the same as before, with a firm build and healthy tan, though his face was older, almost dignified. He had wrinkles in places Annie didn't usually think of as wrinkling: at the tops of his cheeks, and across his nose when he smiled, which he was right now. When he cocked his head, the afternoon sun highlighted where the skin between his ear and neck sagged. Annie wondered what changes the sun revealed about her. All she knew was that it felt wonderful on her bare shoulders, on her scalp, heat being absorbed through her dark hair, her dark jeans. The tube top hugged her lovingly.

Ben said that he was in town for just two days, since he lived in Chicago now, had for the past four years. He told Annie things that she didn't even hear; she was busy being amused by the fact that she had once believed—truly believed—that she would be with this person for the rest of her life.

They proceeded into a bar with windows that opened out onto the street. While panhandlers and drug dealers did their business a few yards away, Annie and Ben had three margaritas each, since summer was finally here and it was that kind of evening—especially in the city, where June was really the only truly enjoyable month of the season. Then Ben offered to walk her home and, when she told him she had moved back to Brooklyn, asked if he could "see" her "place." They both knew what that meant, and so Annie broke another of Caleb Crantz's edicts and, taking Ben with her, rode the subway home.

Though she'd had sex with him many, many times before,

doing so yet again made clear to her that even a photographic memory could not fully recall a person's body, or the things he liked, or the way the parts of him worked, or any of the important information, really. She had to figure things out all over again, and so the episode was something of an ordeal and hardly satisfactory. And now she had to lie here on the still-moist sheets and listen to him bellowing a Hall and Oates song in her shower.

Well, she reasoned to herself, pulling the sheet up across her waist, the last time we did this I was a completely different person. Back then I was angry all the time. I barely had my own life. Now I have a job I like and a schedule that suits my needs. I'm studying for a Ph.D. I have my own runty little apartment, without a roommate, without a husband (without proper heating or insulation—but that was another issue). Back then I'd never slept with anyone else; now I know what all is out there.

She had made it through those first awkward throes of women's liberation, survived the confusion and the fury. This was a new decade. Annie placed a pillow behind her neck and gave the curls of her perm an encouraging little squeeze. When the phone rang, she grabbed the receiver and said, "Yep!"

"Annie Blechinger?"

"That's me."

"Ah, Annie, is Magda. I am calling to see how the revitalizing cream is working."

Well, now, this was a surprise. Annie sat up and turned a guilty eye to the congregation of small but substantial-looking glass bottles atop her bureau. Magda from the Erno Laszlo counter had convinced her, in a moment of weakness, that they were going to save her life. That was last week, the day before her birthday, the day that she panicked and bought the Jordache jeans. "Tomorrow I'll be forty," she had explained to Magda, who reigned over the makeup counter in a chic-looking lab coat. "You know how it is. One day you're forty, the next thing you know you're sixty."

And gorgeous Magda, with eyes like Sophia Loren, had nodded gravely and reached for a jar of revitalizing cream.

Now she said, "I want to make sure you are pleased with the results."

Annie looked at the bottles that sat waiting on her bureau and felt the full burden of ownership. She noted how a simple bit of sexual tussling seemed to take care of the ills all those bottles claimed to cure. She said, "The truth is, Magda, I'm going to have to return most of this crap."

"You are unhappy with the products?"

"I hate to tell you this, but I haven't even used them. I haven't even opened them up."

"Not even the revitalizing cream? You will like it, I guarantee. I call you in a month, when you see how you like it." Magda hung up before Annie could say another word, while Ben's voice floated from the bathroom. *You've got the body, now you want my soul. . . .* He was shutting the water off.

So that was how these makeup counters worked, Annie thought as she replaced the receiver in its cradle. They found you a product and hounded you at home, to make sure you were hooked for life. She had been aware even as she was buying them that the creams were a mistake. They were nothing she could afford, and she'd had to break Caleb Crantz's rules to lug them home. But now that she was forty she knew better. Never again would she cave in like that.

I can't go for that, no, no—no can do. . . .

Well, all right, she would. Of course she would. But wasn't that life? A series of lapses. Like the margaritas and the subway ride and Ben here in her shower. Mistakes were things you made over and over again. You had to forgive yourself. No one could play by *all* the rules. Annie certainly never had.

Ben stopped singing and emerged from the bathroom rubbing a washcloth over his wet hair. "What a picture you make, Annie. You have such a great shape."

He came toward her, naked, smiling the same square-jawed smile he had employed repeatedly to get basically whatever he wanted. Yet he wasn't a bad person; Annie always made that clear, despite continuing to refer to him as "that asshole." She made certain it was understood that that asshole had possessed enough good qualities to keep her hanging around for a good seven years.

Ben sat down on the bed, then rolled onto his side, propped up on an elbow to face her. "I was thinking, in the shower, about that time in the Poconos. When it snowed all day. Remember?"

Annie smiled, a bit wickedly. "And you made us walk all the way around that goddamn lake just so we could feel like we'd done something besides fuck all day." She gave him a tiny shove and then admitted, "Yeah, that was fun."

"And the snowflakes covered your hair," Ben said. "They were so thick and coming down so fast, they didn't melt right away, and I looked at you with your hair all white and thought, That's what she'll look like when she's eighty years old, so beautiful, with long white hair."

Annie pulled herself up on the backs of her arms. "Aw, Ben." And then, trying not to sound annoyed, "You never told me that."

"It was just an image," Ben said, shrugging his shoulders slightly. "I believed it."

Annie looked into his eyes to see if he were telling the truth. Though they were still a bright gray, his eyes were somehow different from before. It wasn't just the crow's-feet. There was more depth to them, Annie could have sworn it. How had that happened?

She said, "Aren't you lucky I ran into you today."

"I am." And then he asked, "So—are you going to tell Eileen?"

Annie gave a loud, squawking laugh. People had told her it sounded obnoxious, but she didn't care. "Is that what you want to know, then? Is that all you're worried about?"

"I just meant—"

"I can't believe you still care what she thinks."

Ben had never liked Eileen, who was Annie's best friend from college and wasn't easy to impress. He said it was because Annie told her everything and in doing so had turned Eileen against him, but Annie knew the real reason. Ben couldn't stand the fact that Eileen was the one woman who had never fallen for his handsomeness.

That's the way it was with men like Ben, who had grown up cute and had nothing but their looks to lose, who could wait until they were practically in their forties to settle down, who saw no reason for any woman to tell them no. They expected adulation and didn't know what to do with women like Eileen, who had never been won over by Ben's winking eyes or fawning remarks. She had never even pretended to like him.

Calamity

Ben had always had a whole circuit of admirers he flirted with regularly. Really they were just shopgirls, counter girls, waitresses. It was for them, not Annie, that Ben used to rub gunk into his bangs, pat on cologne, clip the hairs that peeked out from his nostrils. There was the girl in the dry cleaner's, and the woman who cut his hair, and the gal at the deli counter. Ben made his rounds. Sometimes Annie was with him and witnessed as he complimented some teenager on her lovely green eyes. It was one of the things that had become unbearable. But for years Annie had just stood there next to him trying not to notice.

Now she said, "Of course I'm going to tell Eileen. I tell her everything."

Even as she said it, though, she was deciding that she wouldn't. For one thing, it was embarrassing. Also, it might be a fun challenge for Annie to see if she could keep her own secret. Now that she was forty it was probably time she started trying to build some strength of character.

Ben said, "You haven't changed a bit, I see," but not in an especially bitter way.

With his face so close to hers, Annie was able to see now what hadn't been there before, what made his gaze seem deeper. There was fear, that was what it was, written into those lines around his eyes. Fear and loss, because Ben too knew, finally, what it felt like to barely exist for a whole set of younger people. He too knew what it meant to walk into a room and not even be noticed. He who had always turned heads.

Annie closed her eyes to find the lines. This was the anthology from her freshman-year English course back at Bryn Mawr, the print small and uninviting, the paper so thin it often ripped just from the turning of a page. Ah, there it was. Annie opened her eyes and read aloud:

> *"They flee from me that sometime did me seek*
> *With naked foot, stalking in my chamber.*
> *I have seen them gentle, tame, and meek,*
> *That now are wild and do not remember*
> *That sometime they put themselves in danger*
> *To take bread at my hand; and now they range,*
> *Busily seeking with a continual change."*

She stopped there, and looked Ben in the eye. This poor vain man—he probably had more to lose, even, than she did. After all, he had known what real power felt like, and now it was drifting away. Crow's-feet, some white in his hair, love handles at his waist . . . Was that all it took for him to finally become, like Annie herself, new and improved?

Annie looked at the regiment of bottles lined up on her bureau. She wondered if Ben might want that revitalizing cream. She could offer to sell it to him for a reduced price. But now it was Ben who closed his eyes and spoke:

> *"I knew a woman, lovely in her bones,*
> *When small birds sighed, she would sigh back at them;*
> *Ah, when she moved, she moved more ways than one:*
> *The shapes a bright container can contain!*
> *Of her choice virtues only gods should speak,*
> *Or English poets who grew up on Greek*
> *(I'd have them sing in chorus, cheek to cheek.)"*

Ben stopped. He opened his eyes. His jaw was tight and square, and he seemed to be challenging Annie, as if this were some sort of duel.

He had always liked poetry—had used it to seduce Annie on their first date—yet it shocked her to think he still had a stash of lines ready to offer. And ones as generous as this, ones she had never heard before.

Annie told him, "I'm impressed." Really what she meant was, That was sweet of you.

"And if I didn't know your little secret," Ben said, "I'd be impressed, too." With his forefinger, he gave her a tap on the top of her head.

Annie decided to shift onto her stomach, to give Ben a good view of her broad rump. When he said nothing, she asked, "So—when do you go back to Chicago?"

"Tomorrow afternoon."

He didn't sound regretful, but he didn't sound anxious, either. Annie searched his face, to see if he was eager to leave. While he was in the shower, singing, she had supposed she wanted him to go as soon as possible, but now that he was next to her again, his skin so fresh and moist and clean, it seemed a shame to have brought him all the way back here and not even had very good sex.

Plus, she wouldn't see him again for a long, long time. Probably forever.

This didn't seem sad. Annie almost sat up with the shock of it. She wondered if she could trust her own feelings. She wondered if she would think back on this day years and years from now, or if it would melt away into the atmosphere like so many other days.

She made a decision, and she told herself: *Memorize this.*

Annie looked at Ben and took a photograph with her eyes. Then she moved across his body and straddled him firmly. "Are you sure you live in Chicago? You don't just live right over on that island there?"

Ben said, "You know I don't," and Annie said, "Well, then, in that case we'd better give this one more try."

All Life's Grandeur

The summer I turned thirteen, my father fell in love. At least, that was what I thought; later I learned he and Shirley had already spent two years sleeping together in various hotel rooms, dodging their spouses and sons and early-morning checkouts. But that summer, freshly divorced, they lay on the veranda of the little cottage massaging cocoa oil into each other's shoulders, interspersing conversation with kisses on the neck and earlobes.

My mother was off at her parents' house, "recovering." In fact she was taking pills, lying on the living room floor all day with her head under the coffee table. That's what they told us later. I was focused on my own problems: my body doing things I'd not expected. My voice had finally stabilized in a new, lower register, but the hair on my legs kept growing. And then there were the frequent, boisterous erections. Though the temperature was at least eighty degrees every day, and though no one came to visit us—we knew nobody in that summer town—I always wore jeans around the cottage, removing them only when I decided to enter the frigid river.

I was thin and flat-footed, arches limp as dead trout. When I came shivering out of the water, my footprints left oval splashes on the dock. The wood was dry and splintered. Neglect had loosed the giant nails that held it together, inched them out like rusty mushrooms. You had to be careful not to trip on them or step between the planks; some of the gaps could swallow your ankle whole. Others were narrower, filled with spiders and purple-topped weeds.

To one side of the dock, a bay had formed, with sand soft as mud. It felt like a silk pillow when I waded there, bending down to catch guppies in my hands. Where the water ended, the ground was dark and mossy, with frogs that sat there and never blinked. To the other side of the dock, the shoreline was pebbles, the kind that call for rubber soles. Some nights Dad and Shirley would build bonfires there, and I'd hear Shirley say how she wished *her* Geoff were with us; she was sure we would get along. In blatant inconsideration, she had named her son Geoff, too. At least his was spelled with a "J." He was only eight and lived with his dad in Schenectady.

I just left the two of them alone. I read mysteries and swam, and worried about my body. In yellow swim trunks, I would wrap a long towel around my waist to walk to the dock. My father laughed at me, and Shirley said, "Oh, honey."

. . .

I was lying on the dock one afternoon in early July, sun-drying after a swim, when a stranger caught me towel-less. "How much'll you give for these worms?"

I quickly covered myself. A few feet away was a suntanned girl, her wispy brown hair pulled back in a plastic clip. She was still skinny the way little kids are, legs like sticks, over which she wore denim shorts with turtle patches on the pockets. Her flip-flops were orange and her tank suit green, her bony shoulders poking out from the straps. She seemed a whole world younger than the girls in seventh grade, who wore eyeshadow and some-times bras. "Your dad said I'd find you down here," she told me. "He said you might be interested."

"In what?"

"Worms. You fish, don't you? I've seen you fishing from the dock, and in your canoe. I live up there." She pointed vaguely upstream. "Hanlam's Bay. See that little gray house by the com-munal dock? Next to the one with the motorboat. That's where I live. With the grass and trees up top. We're neighbors." She tilted her head and squinted at me. "So how about it? You want some worms?"

As she well knew, worms were a hot commodity in that sum-mer haven. The only place to buy any was Arno's Live Bait, which entailed a trip into town and a venture into the dark, raw-smelling rowhouse that was Arno's home and business. I'd never actually seen Arno, and possibly he no longer existed, for the enterprise appeared to be entirely in the hands of his descendants. There were innumerable Arno juniors: picking their noses out on the stoop, swatting flies on the front porch, playing tag in the living room, or watching TV in the kitchen, where one of them would open an enormous refrigerator to fetch you your half-price maggots. All had the same pale freckles, thin brown hair, and sweaty faces and appeared to never leave their crowded home. They were their own gang, and I had never liked dealing with them. This girl seemed to know it. "Where'd you get yours?" I asked her.

"It's a secret."

I let out a bored breath. "How much you want for them?"

The girl held her head up high and said, "They're free if you'll take me out in your canoe."

From the veranda above, my father stood with Shirley, hands around each other's waists, nodding down at me.

That was how it started. I think it wasn't until we were already out in the boat, spearing plump earthworms on hooks, that we thought to ask each other's names. Hers was Valerie. We sat there under the four-o'clock sun and guided our fishing rods patiently.

"How old are you?" I asked.

"Eleven."

I wanted to tell Valerie that I had entered a world to which she was not yet privy, one where you had to change classrooms and teachers for each subject, and clothes for gym. Some kids smoked in the bathrooms, and my best friend, Mack, had even procured a few *Playboys*, which had been passed around covertly and scrutinized reverently.

But with her flat chest and narrow hips Valerie did not even seem worthy of such information. I just sighed and tried to look dissatisfied.

"A boy drowned right about here," Valerie said. She shrugged a shoulder and managed to look somehow embarrassed. "He got caught in the seaweed. There's parts out here where it's like an underground jungle, a whole underwater tropical rain forest, and if you get caught in it, the weeds grab your legs and hold you under." Valerie's pale eyes shot me a challenging look. "That's why my mom won't let me swim out here."

"I can swim wherever I want."

"Well, fine, you may be allowed to swim wherever you want, but don't say I didn't warn you." Valerie gave a little huff. "Why do you keep that towel wrapped around your legs?"

I'd heard it on commercials: "Sensitive skin."

Valerie showed up at the cottage every day, and Dad and Shirley were always there to smile and nod and make sure that I joined her. Here I was, ready for my first summer romance, saddled with an eleven-year-old who for all I knew still believed in Santa Claus. Though my romantic fantasies were embarrassingly ignorant (even after what I'd learned in science class, the most I could imagine was a prolonged kiss, unaware of the fact that tongues were involved), they made no allowances for preteens. I pictured myself with some big-breasted girl, walking hand in hand to buy ice cream, licking from each other's cones.

Instead I had scrawny Valerie. We swam, canoed, and played cards on the old dock, which Valerie preferred to the communal one she and her neighbors shared in Hanlam's Bay. She showed me the cool, shady area behind her parents' place where she dug for worms, and we went fishing regularly. This was way out in the middle of nowhere, don't forget; there weren't any other kids my age nearby. If I were back home, Mack and I would have been riding our bikes to the pool, or playing Atari, or exploring the tunnels under the library without our mothers' knowing. I took opportunities to remind Valerie of this. I made sure she understood that our friendship would never have occurred had my father not met Shirley, my mother not—after threatening to use a razor blade on herself— been sent off to her parents, and I not been dragged to some small cottage where I knew no one.

At least twice a week we rode our bikes into town to see a movie at the Ascott Theatre, a dilapidated establishment that appeared to be owned by a grim-looking man and his dog. The dog, a Doberman, wore a spiked collar and barked at anyone who entered the premises, which explained the low turnout. That and the fact that the movies weren't current; they were old ones, sometimes classics but most of the time just old. You needed a car to get to the multiplex, three towns over.

In the lobby of the theater was a brown card table, on top of which sat a fishbowl. Propped against it was a scrawled notice that asked patrons to place their business cards in the bowl. WIN A THOUSAND BUCKS, read a separate, menacing sign below. No "dollars" and no exclamation point—more like an order that the grim man and the angry dog were there to ensure. "Winner selected end of August," a lowercase jotting concluded. Even then I didn't understand how they could be giving away a thousand dollars when the theater was in such bad shape. The red vinyl seats had huge holes in them, and the screen was missing a curtain on one side.

The fishbowl was nearly empty in early July, but a week later a few business cards had been added. Valerie and I checked up on the bowl every time we went to the theater. Valerie would pick out a card to see who went there besides us. She usually made fun of whoever's card it was. "Charles Lampert, Chiropractor. Just call him Mr. Backcracker. That's what a chiropractor does; they have you lie down, and then they sit on you, to crack your back. Good old fat Charles Lampert." She tossed the card back in the bowl.

"Get your prissy hands outta there." That was what the grim man usually said. Other times he was sparring with his Doberman and didn't notice.

"One day that man's dog is going to die and he'll have no one left to play with," Valerie said once when we were sitting in the dark expanse of the theater, waiting out a technical failure. "He'll be stuck in this place all alone." She put a handful of popcorn in her mouth and munched. "I bet that's what the thousand bucks is for. I bet there's a condition if you win it: you have to promise to be that man's friend when his dog dies, to hang out here with him and wear that leather collar with the studs. Only then do you get the money."

I don't remember what I said back, because I was preoccupied with the sudden realization that I smelled. I had only recently begun to wash my underarms, and sometimes I forgot to put on deodorant. This was the first time I'd noticed just how powerfully my own body's secretions could make themselves known to the world at large. I sat there wondering if Valerie could smell me, or if she was trying to ignore it. This just made me sweat even more. My mistake seemed enormous, unforgivable. I had not yet considered the subtle grades of difference between embarrassment, shame, and guilt.

. . .

On the way back from the movies, we would spy on Arno's Live Bait. It was my idea: now that I had no reason to see them, I sought them out. Valerie would oblige me halfheartedly while I went up to the bushes behind the rowhouse, right up to the kitchen window, to watch what was going on there. The one big sister, older than the rest, was usually taking money from customers and passing them grubby plastic containers from the giant refrigerator. This big girl was pale, fat, and slow-moving, always in bare feet, shorts, and a stained T-shirt, gently scolding one or another of her younger siblings, and watching whichever soap opera was on television. One day, as I watched her haul herself out of a chair to help a customer, I realized that she was pregnant. Her protruding belly was not just fat—it was full of another life altogether. I found this fact horrifying and immediately suggested we leave. Valerie, as always, seemed relieved; when it came to the Arnos, the only thing she showed much enthusiasm for was throwing mini-firecrackers at their house—those little ones that make a "bang" sound when they hit. She took some from her pocket and, as we went on our way, aimed them against the side wall.

Part of the reason I was so disgusted by the pregnant girl was the thought of what was occurring to her body, and part of it had to do with the day, a week or so earlier, that I'd come home to hear my father having sex with Shirley. I had said goodbye to Valerie after returning from town, and when I got back to our little cottage, Dad and Shirley were not on the veranda like normal. When I went inside I heard moaning sounds I recognized from

Calamity

34

movies (not the ones we saw at the Ascott). I quickly went back out to the dock, where I sat and thought of my mother. This same thing had gone on between him and her, too—my mother, who had in the past year cried more tears than I thought it possible to even possess. Everything seemed utterly wrong. What if Shirley got pregnant, like the Arno sister? In school the previous year, we had been shown film strips emphasizing that all upcoming changes in a girl's body were for the ultimate purpose of pregnancy and childbirth. These were fuzzy recordings meant to debunk sexual myths and provide necessary factual information, and for months afterward Mack and I had repeated, inexhaustibly, some of our favorite lines: "In some primitive cultures, the menstruating female is thought to turn milk sour." "As each egg matures, it BURSTS from the ovary." "Fat is deposited on the hips, and nipples stand out." These phrases never failed to make us collapse in laughter. Now, though, I just felt queasy. Valerie's wispy shape would change soon, too, I found myself thinking. We had been shown the film strips separately from the girls, and as a result I could never look at girls the same again.

Valerie went into Reed's grocery across the street to buy her Fireballs, but I told her I'd wait outside. Instead I found myself going back to the Arnos' window, for one more glimpse at the pregnant sister. I peeked my head over the sill to find her staring back at me.

"Where's Val?" the sister asked in a surprisingly soft voice. I froze.

"She okay?" the sister went on. "Is she doing all right?"

"Sure," I said. "She's fine."

"You tell her we miss her," the girl said. "I was never close with her, but I always liked her. You can tell her I said that."

"Okay," I said, turning away. I ran across to the grocery, where Valerie was waiting in line. She was holding a plastic pack of big red candy FireBalls, but she opened her front pocket discreetly to make sure I saw she had stolen three packs of chewing gum.

"Getting a Charleston Chew?" she asked innocently.

My face flared red with guilt that wasn't even mine. The flat-chested pipsqueak—I could have turned her in right there. But I wasn't yet ready to enter, or even to acknowledge, the world of betrayal. It sufficed to keep secret the conversation I had just had.

After the afternoon that I walked in on Dad and Shirley, I tried to convince Valerie to let us spend less time at my place and more at hers—a one-story house with a porch behind it that looked onto a small grassy area. The house was bigger and sturdier than our rented cottage, since Valerie's family lived there year-round. They didn't have a lot of money, Valerie often reminded me. She said this was because her father was a poet.

I had never met a poet before. After knowing Valerie's father, I was under the impression, for years to come, that poets were unconditionally cheerful people. "Hey-hey!" he always greeted us, swooping Valerie up in his arms. "Still a lightweight," he would say, putting her back down and pretending to be disappointed. "You've gotta put some meat on your bones."

He filled in silences with jolly talk. "Geoff, Valerie," he might say in mock seriousness, "I want each of you to eat one of

these nectarines. And then I want you to tell me: is life good?"
And he would hand us each a perfectly ripe nectarine. His jovial
face seemed to be a balance against Mrs. Darden's, which had
something sad about it. When Mr. Darden joked, she gave wist-
ful smiles.

"I just met your parents downtown," she said to me one hot
afternoon as the four of us lounged on their porch. I was in my
swim trunks, concentrating on not raising my arms too high;
overnight, it seemed, the hairs there had thickened into a patch
of dark-brown fur.

"You mean my dad and Shirley," I corrected. "My mother's
in Fenton with my grandparents."

"Recovering," Valerie added, and I wished I hadn't confided
in her.

Mrs. Darden turned and surprised me with a flicker of
something in her eyes. But it quickly subsided, and she said,
"Oh." She put her hand on my back and said softly, "We all re-
cover at some point."

"Listen to this," Mr. Darden said, almost impatiently, ad-
justing himself on the wicker recliner. "Some Robert Lowell for
your listening pleasure." And he read:

"O to break loose. All life's grandeur
is something with a girl in summer . . ."

The rest of the stanza didn't make much sense to me, even
though Mr. Darden read it in a clear, triumphant tone. Then he
slapped the book closed and laughed. "You'll read the rest later.
Crazy genius." He shook his head, and Mrs. Darden went quietly
back inside.

. . .

When I arrived back at the cottage later that day, Shirley, tanned and blonder than ever, said, "Mrs. Bloor who runs the bakery told me that Valerie's parents lost a child last summer. Valerie's brother. He drowned when Valerie and her parents were in town one day."

I pretended not to hear. I still felt distant enough from Shirley not to have to speak to her. But she went on. "He and two of the sons from the Live Bait store were out in a summer boy's sailboat. The weather got rough, and the boat capsized. Valerie's brother must have hit his head. The other boys lived. It was just one of those freak accidents."

"So it's a good thing you've been playing with her," my father added. "I'm sure it takes her mind off things. You keep it up."

I was old enough to resent a father's orders. I wanted to tell him how Valerie pocketed candy without paying, how she threw firecrackers at the Arno house. I wanted to remind him that if it weren't for him and Shirley I could have been home with kids my age, with Mack who understood me, with my mother who loved me more than anyone else and certainly more than some blonde smiling woman with painted toenails and her hand on my father's butt.

My days with Valerie now felt even more like a responsibility. I couldn't help running through my head, daily, that stormy scenario: a sailboat tossed by wind and waves, rain pounding water, three boys thrashing, maybe yelling, maybe not. It wasn't something I wanted to think about, but Valerie was a constant re-

Calamity

38

minder. I resented her misfortune, and her eleven-year-old-ness. Where were those carefree teenage girls that I now, more than ever, felt ready to take on?

By late August I no longer thought twice about the hair under my arms, was no longer ashamed of my autonomous erections. I even convinced myself I'd grown bigger biceps. I was looking forward to getting back to school, to Mack and our Red Sox bets, to girls with hips, away from Dad and Shirley, home to my mother, who—according to a call from my grandmother—was "doing a little better."

On the way to the Ascott Theatre with Valerie two days before I was to leave, I stopped into Reed's grocery to buy my usual Charleston Chew. They froze them for you there, if you liked them that way. When I came back outside, I saw Valerie staring at Arno's Live Bait across the street, her head tilted shyly down. I walked over to watch the Arnos in action. It was the usual—the young ones fighting, playing, and eating sandwiches, their grimy fingers leaving dirt marks on the cheap white bread. All of it was what I, an only child, had never had the opportunity to experience: brothers stealing pickles out of sisters' hands, the littlest boy carelessly knocking into an older sibling's calf, one girl leaning against another, who braided the filthy hair of a third. Sweaty young bodies, stomachs peeking out from handed-down hand-me-downs. The pregnant girl was there, fanning herself on the front stoop. She waved at us. An older brother sat down next to her and, seeing us nearby, called, "Hi, Val," in a shy voice.

"Hi," Valerie called back, and then, turning to me, said, "Let's go." When we began walking away, she said, "I hate them. I hate them more than anything."

"Why? What have they done to you?" I said this despite

what I knew—that they had done nothing other than continue to live.

And, as if she too knew this, Valerie said, head down, "Nothing."

But when we entered the old theater she still seemed angry. The Doberman growled at us. Valerie said, "Let's go up to the balcony and spit on people."

It wasn't anything I felt like doing. To divert Valerie, I went up to the fishbowl, which had gradually produced a small pile of business cards, and said, "Who will it be today?" I picked out a card and read, "Alida Hayes. *Total Body Beauty*. Hair, nails, waxing, European facials."

Valerie looked up and let her shoulders unhunch. "Let's call her," she said.

"What do you mean?"

"Let's call her up. On the phone." She grabbed the card from my hand. "Her number's right here: 489-7623."

"Why do you want to call her?"

"To tell her she *won*, stupid."

"You mean prank her?"

"You'll have to do it," Valerie said, suddenly businesslike. "Since your voice sounds older."

It seemed like it could be funny. Like when we'd call up random numbers and ask whoever answered what they wanted on their pizza. I laughed. "Sure."

There was a pay phone in front of the theater, and we did it right there. When I told her she'd won, Alida Hayes started screaming. It was a long, multi-toned scream interspersed with the words "thank you" and lasted a good forty-five seconds. I'd never had anyone thank me so heartily, so gratefully. Then Alida Hayes said, "For once I can finally go on vacation!"

I hadn't expected this. I felt my heart drop the way it had the night my mom found out about Dad and Shirley. Of course I hadn't known what Mom had found out, but I'd known something was wrong, just as I did right now.

Alida Hayes asked, "When should I come pick it up—the check, I mean? It's a check, right? I hope so, because I'd like to reserve a ticket—"

"We'll bring it over to you," I said quickly. Valerie was tapping me on the shoulder, mouthing, "What's she saying?"

"Oh, great!" Alida Hayes was saying. "Wonderful! Will the paper be covering this? I mean, will there be a photograph or anything?"

"Uh—yes, ma'am."

"Well, oh my—could you possibly wait a half-hour or so? Because I'd like to do my hair."

"N-no problem," I stuttered. Valerie stuck her ear next to the receiver.

"Oh, wonderful," said Alida Hayes. "Thank you, thank you so much!"

"You're welcome." I hung up, my hands shaking.

"What'd she say?" Valerie asked quickly. "What'd she do?"

"Oh—nothing really," I managed to say.

"What do you mean?" Valerie sounded annoyed.

"It didn't really work."

That was enough of an explanation for Valerie, who tossed Alida Hayes' business card on the sidewalk, saying, "Race you to Reed's—winner buys FireBalls!"

All Life's Grandeur

When Valerie came by the cottage the next day, I couldn't look at her. I stared out at the river, where sea scum basked on the surface. There had been a morning storm. "I'm not feeling well," I told Valerie, until she went home. I was trying not to picture Alida Hayes, what her hair looked like after she had fixed it up and waited for the newspaper crew to show. I supposed that after a long enough time she would have called the theater and learned the truth. Valerie didn't come by again until that evening. "C'mon, let's make a bonfire," she said, when I'd been ignoring her for an hour. I told her I had to do family things with my dad. Of course, he just spent the night rubbing Shirley's feet, and I played battleship against myself, which, for the record, doesn't work.

That was my last full day at the cottage. The next morning Valerie came to say goodbye and found me again sitting on the edge of the dock. Wisps of seaweed nodded in the water. "You'll be starting school next week, huh?" Valerie asked.

"Yup," I said. "I don't mind."

"Will you miss me?" she asked. "Will you think of me?"

"Sure," I said. But the summer was already taking the shape of a degraded memory, to be pushed aside and back. I said, "I hope I make the soccer team."

"I'll think of you," Valerie said. "You'll ask your dad to come back here next summer, right?"

"I just remembered something I forgot to pack."

"Well, let me give you my address and phone number." Valerie took a little pink address book from her pocket. She had already written her information on a piece of paper, which she handed to me, and then had me fill mine in on a page in her little book. "Well, I guess this is so long, for now," she said.

"So long," I said, as she opened her arms wide. It was not a gesture I was prepared for; the girls I knew didn't hug. Valerie stepped back when she noticed my hesitation, but she didn't lower her arms. I stepped into them, and we hugged each other goodbye, but all I could think was that here I finally had a chance to touch a girl and she was only eleven.

Valerie turned to leave. "I'll keep my fingers crossed for you to make the soccer team," she said as she walked away.

Back home, I forgot all about Valerie. There were more important things to attend to: soccer, schoolwork, masturbation. I spent a lot of time in my room rather than face my mother, who, as evidence of her recovery, smiled extremely at all times. It was a tight, frightening smile that she had never had before, and it was accompanied by spurts of enthusiasm for the minutest activity. "The *weather* was so *beautiful* today, I just had to pull *weeds!*" she would say when I returned on a Sunday night after spending the weekend with Dad and Shirley. That choke-hold grin. She would answer the phone, prepare dinner, clean the kitchen with ferocious glee.

I stopped inviting friends over. To me it was the ultimate betrayal, my mother having replaced herself with this grinning dull-eyed woman. My father told me it must be medication, and when I asked her point-blank, my mother confirmed it. "The medicine fixes my mood so that I can find the energy to deal with the *problem*," she explained brightly. "How can I fix the *problem* if I'm in a bad *mood*?"

In November she checked herself into The Hillsbrook Retreat, and I went to live with my father and Shirley and Shirley's son, who must have worn out his welcome in Schenectady. It wasn't until December that I received a letter Valerie had written over a month earlier, telling me about her school and asking if I'd made the soccer team. The very concept of mail being forwarded was nothing I'd ever had the opportunity to consider. The fact that the letter managed to find me—and at such an improbable location, the house where my father and Shirley cohabited—seemed meaningful, ominous. The whole glum summer, which I had successfully forgotten, came back to me. Not the big things, like the reason for Mrs. Darden's weak smile or Valerie's loneliness, or the fact that I would never write her back. But everything else: the Arno clan, the Doberman, Mr. Darden reading poetry aloud. I even dreamed that I ran into Alida Hayes. She was crying, her hair in a stiff bouffant, saying, "They never showed up." Then she turned into my old third grade teacher and yelled at me for cheating on my math test, which really happened, even though I hadn't cheated. Then I woke up and promised God I would somehow call Alida Hayes back in the morning and apologize, but I didn't.

Anyway, it may not sound so important now, but it's why, when my father pulled me aside one evening during my mother's months away and said, "I'm sorry, so very sorry, to have put you through this," I forgave him. "You don't know what it feels like," he said to me. "You don't know the guilt." I thought of Valerie—who had, despite her youth, known this adulthood before me—and said, "I know."

Prom Season

In French class their teacher, Madame Lipsky, made an announcement: "Prom is one and a half months from today, and I want you boys to ensure that every girl in this room has a date. None of this 'I'm going stag' garbage. No more 'I'm too cool to go to the prom' baloney. I don't want a single girl telling me she hasn't been invited just because you boys are too wimpy to pick up the phone, dial a number, and ask her." Madame Lipsky peered gravely over the broad plastic rims of her glasses. "It's your duty. *Entendu?*"

The boys nodded sullenly and gave her their word. From his seat in the back row, Mack felt, already, the heavy weight of an unfinished task. Though he regularly left assignments until the last minute and rarely felt pressure to do well on any of them, what Madame Lipsky wanted was greater than just Mack and his report card; suddenly there were all these girls—and not just his mother—to disappoint.

"So much for our plans," Geoff, Mack's best friend, muttered, though they'd made no plans. At least, Mack hadn't. They spent after-school hours eating bubbly slices at Palazzo Pizza, stealing dumb things from the Woolworth's, thumbing through used albums at J.J.'s Records & Cassettes. Though their town was a mere subway line away from Cambridge and downtown Boston, they were perfectly comfortable just loitering at the deli or smoking pot and playing video games at Carl Loam's house. Theirs was a school full of people who seldom rode anything other than a car or bicycle, who spent weekend hours in backyards and malls and multi-screen cinemas. Some of the kids might go to Harvard Square to hang out at the Pit, but Mack and Geoff mostly did things like play Frisbee with whoever happened to be at the park. None of these things required planning. In fact, the only thing Mack had ever done that took any serious attention was write his application for college—a small, nondescript one in Connecticut, to which he had since been accepted.

A note, crumpled into a stiff ball, landed on Mack's little kidney-shaped desk. He knew it was from Tilda and unfolded it with mild curiosity.

"DO YOUR DUTY, BOY!"

It would never have occurred to anyone to not do what Madame Lipsky had asked. For one thing, she was sure to be grading them on it. That was the way her classes worked, and it was the reason students liked her. Her system made it possible to succeed simply by volunteering for the multiple-sclerosis walk she organized each autumn, or by being nice to Jessica

Schneck (who had tried to commit suicide two years ago and, unfortunately for everyone else, failed). This system was to everyone's advantage. On the broadest level, it fostered an aura of good will that radiated from Madame Lipsky's French classes to permeate the rest of the high school. Administrators sometimes said that there was more humanity in Madame Lipsky's classroom than in the rest of the world—which was probably why they kept Madame Lipsky on even though no one from her classes had ever even attempted to take the Advanced Placement exam.

That was because, on a more basic level, Madame Lipsky's system meant that you needn't actually speak any French. Madame Lipsky didn't. She passed class time letting her students watch videos that had anything French in them—a character with a French name, say, or a scene in a French restaurant—and for every film of the students' choosing she would retaliate with a selection of her own. Since she was the teacher, her choices didn't even need to have a French element. After the students selected *The Pink Panther*, for instance, she had them watch *Legal Eagles* because, she said, "I just love how they've done Debra Winger's hair."

To Mack and the others, this was all part of a public school education, and they were grateful for Madame Lipsky's straight talk. It was refreshing to be treated like mature beings, if not full-fledged adults. Most of the other teachers had given up long ago and greeted each incoming class as though witnessing an influx of carpenter ants. Either that or they were young and overeager, composed rhyming ballads about math formulas, made profuse apologies for ungraded exams—were embarrassing in their enthusiasm for things that surely meant nothing in the greater world. Mack and the others couldn't help assuming that what they learned in Madame Lipsky's class was of more use than the usual high school fare. There was little doubt that the way Madame Lipsky ran things was the way the real world worked.

Madame Lipsky's announcement marked the official start of prom season. Within days students were discussing cummerbunds and boutonnieres and whose house to escape to afterward. To Mack it felt like an approaching storm, or an exam or a trial. He had attended two school dances before, the kind where the girls asked the boys, and both times it had been an ordeal, dressing up in rented suits that made him feel like someone in a play, meeting the parents of a girl he barely knew and didn't really want to go out with again, while his mother laughed at him and at his crooked bow tie and snapped photographs that were sure to be used in some sort of blackmail years and years from now.

But none of those past dances could match the Senior Prom, which at this point in the year was the only thing to hold the seniors' attention. They were about to graduate and already knew where they'd be going to college or working. Their grades barely mattered anymore. Nothing could match the drama of who had found a dress and who almost had but it wasn't the right size, of who would carpool with whom, and who was spending the weekend at the Cape afterward. But Mack found the hype off-putting—and so Mack put it off.

Geoff, on the other hand, immediately took Madame Lipsky's order to heart and, in typical fashion, asked Leslie Murphy, the one girl you could safely take to a dance without being suspected of having a crush on her. Leslie was extremely smart and perfectly fine-looking without being pretty and wore skirts only three times a year, for the choral concerts in December and May and for the annual awards ceremony, where she tended to win all the prizes. Mack could almost see Geoff—who in all three of his college letters of recommendation had been described as "responsible"—checking her off some mental list. Geoff always completed his objectives swiftly and smartly, which was why the teachers loved him and how he had gotten into Pomona.

The teachers loved Mack, too, but in a slightly exasperated way that Mack found comforting. He used to think that their affection for him was due to his mother, who everyone knew had raised him on her own yet attended parent-teacher conferences with none of the belligerence or accusatory concern of so many other parents. Geoff said that Mack's mother was especially great because even though she made it clear Mack ought to be working harder and getting better grades she actually just let him do whatever he wanted (which meant that Mack had never been particularly rebellious at all).

As for the prom, Mack supposed he should ask Tilda. She often spent time with him and Geoff at Carl Loam's house, and he was used to her sarcasm and her long spurts of laughter. She was basically one of the guys, except that she wasn't. She was a girl, and this was impossible to ignore, especially when she wore that green knit sweater that was just slightly too small. Tilda was tall, like Mack, with a big, somewhat horsy smile and a mess of reddish hair that she barely bothered to comb. Now that the weather was hot, she kept wearing shorts to school. There had been one steamy day, a year before, when Mack looked over and saw she'd hiked her rayon skirt up above her knees, onto her thighs.

That image returned to him often, the fabric piled there lightly across her freckled flesh. There were plenty of other images around to tantalize him—the postcards in Carl Loam's room, for instance—but it was the memory of Tilda with her skirt piled up that always set Mack off.

Plus, he liked Tilda, truly—more than any other girl. The problem was, she had an even bigger crush (it was obvious) on him, and that was always a bit of a turnoff.

Each afternoon, during seventh period, in Fourth Year French, Madame Lipsky held an update. She looked at everyone through those huge, tinted glasses, from under her huge, tinted hair, and said, Whoever doesn't have a date yet, raise your hand. She was in her forties and wore shoulder pads in all of her blouses, which usually tied in floppy bows at the neck. Her skirts were always long, and her leather boots scrunched down around her heels like the skin on a bulldog's face. She wore bright rouge and eyeshadow and slightly purple lipstick. Somehow, on Madame Lipsky, this combination looked perfectly acceptable.

Already people were pairing off. Bernard Leeson, who would do anything for an A, within a week had asked Jessica Schneck. Even girls who hadn't yet been asked were spending hours after school at Nancy's Look Great! Shop, examining rainbows of eye-shadow, requesting special antiperspirant for delicate fabrics, researching nail polish and face powder and adhesive cups that could keep anyone's breasts perky under a strapless dress for up to eighteen hours. There were lipsticks that doubled as blush, and hair rollers you heated up before clipping them in. Mack heard all about these innovations during gym class, where, adorned in team pinnies soaked with the previous classes' sweat, the girls formed little gangs in the outfield to discuss whether they wanted baby's breath or ivy in their corsages.

When it came to boys like Mack, Madame Lipsky appeared to

expect them to take their time. But one Friday she told the class, "We have a problem."

The students braced themselves for another assignment.

Carmine Bocchino, Madame Lipsky explained, had asked five girls and still didn't have a date.

Carmine wasn't even in their French class. He had a speech impediment and was in the "slow" track. But the kids in the "slow" track were constantly picking on him, because he was short and scrawny and talked funny. And so he didn't really have any friends. In fact, no one had ever given him any thought at all until the business about the prom.

Within minutes it was clear to everyone in Fourth Year French what the problem was: Carmine had reached far out of his league. First he had asked Natalie Lopez, the editor of the school paper, who was petite and extremely pretty and not the sort of person even Mack would ever feel comfortable approaching. When Natalie called Carmine the next night to tell him an official No thank you (it had taken her a whole day to formulate a polite, well-worded rejection of just the right tone), Carmine waited approximately two minutes before phoning Trini Prince, who had starred in every single school play except *The Man Who Came to Dinner* (and that was only because she had mononucleosis that semester). Trini, too, asked Carmine if she could call him back, and, after practicing the lines briefly, delivered her refusal in a kindly and optimistic yet firm manner.

At school the next morning, Carmine had cornered Molly Lang, the star of the girls' basketball team (and a good foot taller than Carmine); she told him she was waiting for "a special someone." And so Carmine had moved on to Geraldine Crowley, the head cheerleader, and when she said a flat-out Sorry, no, went straight to Belle Gardner, who was seven months pregnant yet hadn't lost her habit of threatening to beat up anyone who annoyed her. She told Carmine that if he didn't get away from her that second she would beat him up.

All of these facts emerged in a matter of minutes, as the girls of Fourth Year French began sharing information they had promised never to reveal to anyone.

"Natalie told me right afterward; she couldn't believe he had the nerve to ask her."

"Trini was so shocked, she had to rehearse her lines with me."

"Geraldine was totally grossed out; we had to go buy her some aspirin."

"I was right there at my locker when Belle grabbed him by his shirt."

(No one could figure out, though, who Molly Lang's "special someone" might be.)

But with Madame Lipsky so concerned, no one dared make fun of Carmine. No one said he had been foolish to ask all the school's best girls. After all, wasn't he doing what all the boys wished they could? They forgot that they had ever thought of him as ridiculous. His predicament began to seem, even to them, slightly tragic.

Now the Fourth Year French girls who didn't have dates were preparing polite rejections, trying them out on one another, since it seemed you never knew when or where Carmine might pop up. Madame Lipsky told them to shush, to listen up, and to think.

"We need to put our heads together," Madame Lipsky said.

"I'm not asking any of you girls to be Carmine's date, but we need to do some work here. I want you to go home and brainstorm, and let's see what we can come up with."

But as quickly as the problem had arisen, it seemed to disappear. The gossip stopped, the chain of proposals ended, and there were no more Carmine-in-action sightings, no more stories of polite, shocked refusals.

Mack supposed Carmine had given up; that was what Mack would have done. But Geoff said someone must have said yes.

"Nah, you think? To Carmine?"

"Someone must have."

"But *who*?" Everyone wondered. But no one was friends with Carmine, and so no one asked him.

"What about you?" Geoff asked Mack one weekend, when they were out in the woods behind Geoff's father's house, smoking Mack's mother's cigarettes.

"What about me?"

"Have you asked her yet?"

"Asked who what?"

"Tilda. Don't play dumb."

"Should I ask her?"

"Why not? Prom's in two weeks. We can all go hang out at Leslie's aunt's place on the Cape."

Mack tried to pay attention to the thoughts that came into his head. Some of them were images from when he was with Tilda: making that DNA replica for Mr. Bunuel's class, or doing disgusting things with the soup at lunch. Some of them were things she had said to him when they were horsing around, and the times when she had made it obvious how much she liked him. There were images of her neck, which Mack sometimes imagined kissing, and her hips, which he sometimes imagined touching, and the way her cotton shirts sometimes clung to her chest. And then there was the rayon skirt piled across her freckled thighs. Not knowing what else to do, Mack said, "Yeah, I'll ask her tomorrow."

When he did, the next morning, out by the flagpole before the bell rang, Tilda's face dropped and her eyes lowered. She looked annoyed. "I already have a date."

"You do?" This possibility hadn't occurred to Mack, and so he sounded even more incredulous than he felt. "But you never said you did."

"Do I have to tell you everything I do?"

"Who is it?"

"Carmine Bocchino."

Mack laughed. "No, really, who is it?"

"I just told you." Tilda's face was red.

"You've got to be kidding." When she shook her head, Mack said, "You don't even know him."

"He at least asked. He at least had the nerve to come up to me and ask. He didn't wait a whole month because he was too lazy to get off his ass and do something that takes guts."

Tilda looked like she wanted to say more but suddenly turned and walked quickly away. The bell rang, and everyone funneled into the building for the start of yet another day.

The morning was even hotter than usual, and already the classrooms were filled with that stuffy excitement that blows in with the end of the school year. The only thing left was final exams, and yet with weather so sunny it didn't seem exams could possibly matter. Nothing did, this time of year, with flowers sprouting out all over the place and teachers sneezing from hay fever. The heat made it impossible to concentrate, and everyone smelled. All Mack could think about was Tilda. He spent all morning staring out of windows, the air filled with a melancholy scent. He felt something growing inside him, something uncomfortable, unbearable. He thought he might burst.

That afternoon, in seventh period French, Madame Lipsky took the weekly tally—Whoever doesn't have a date, raise your hand. She didn't look surprised at the fact that Mack was the only one with his hand in the air. "What's the problem here? Are you waiting for the moon to be at exactly the right angle? Are you waiting for a drum roll? Are you waiting for a sign from God?"

Mack felt the heat in his cheeks. He said, "The girl I want to take is going with someone else."

He was sweating now. Someone in front of him was snickering. Mack didn't dare look at Tilda to see her reaction.

Madame Lipsky shook her head. "I'm sorry, did I miss something? Is there something someone forgot to tell me? Is there some new policy here?" She walked right up to Mack's desk and said, "Since when does everyone get to go with the person they *want* to take?"

When Mack didn't say anything, she continued. "You are going to a dance. You are going to spend approximately eight hours in the company of a girl who for all I know you won't speak to again after you graduate three weeks from now. There's probably a perfectly nice and deserving girl in another classroom at this very minute just waiting for someone to take her. Since when does it have to be the love of your life?"

Mack felt a trickle of sweat rolling down the side of his torso. He didn't want to ask that perfectly nice and deserving girl. He didn't want to take anyone but Tilda. This was so clear to him that he thought he might shout it.

Instead he spoke in his usual, lax tone. "Why shouldn't it be? If the person's out there and wants to go with me, too, but happens to have already said yes to some dumbass who got to her first, then why can't we shuffle things around? Why do we always have to be punished for our mistakes?"

It wasn't a terribly convincing argument, he knew, but, then, he had never done very well in any of his written essays, either.

Madame Lipsky squinted at him from behind her purple-tinted glasses. "Sometimes we're punished, and sometimes we aren't. But you, young man, have a decision to make."

Mack, though, had made up his mind. He had decided to suffer. Because even suffering was easier than getting up and doing something about it.

After class, when everyone was zipping backpacks and slamming lockers shut for the day, Tilda found him. Her cheeks were red from the heat, and her sweat gave her a healthy shine. "Did you really mean what you said in class today?"

"Which part?"

"The whole thing, I guess."

"Tilda, I'm just kicking myself for not asking you sooner. I know I was dumb. I'm sorry."

Tilda looked down shyly for a moment. In a soft, guilty voice, she said, "I think I might be able to get out of going with Carmine. I mean, I'm sure I can figure something out."

Mack felt his heart leap. He had made a mistake but had been saved. Wasn't that the way it should be? Somehow he wasn't surprised, and he realized that he had expected something like this. His whole life, it seemed, women had come to his rescue—his mother, his grandmother, his teachers. He was accustomed to having things work out.

And so he took it as a matter of course when, that evening, Tilda called to say, in her best hit-man imitation, "Alright, boss, the deed's been done." She sounded jokey, but Mack heard something else behind her voice.

"I'm really glad, Tilda." Mack waited for her to say that she was glad, too, but she changed her tone completely and asked him about the math homework. When he had answered her question, she said a quick Thanks, see you tomorrow, as if the math, and not the prom, were her reason for calling in the first place.

Mack told her goodbye. The feeling that had filled his stomach, that had made him want to burst, was gone.

The next week at school, Mack saw Carmine everywhere. Ahead of him in the lunch line, in the hall between classes, in the parking lot at the end of the day. Always Carmine would look Mack in the eye, a flat, blank look that made Mack's heart pause. He wondered what sort of lie Tilda had made up for Carmine. But when he finally asked her, at her locker one afternoon, she said, briskly, "The truth. You know what they say, honesty, the best policy, blah blah."

She had been this way with him for days now, quick and

dismissive, as if she didn't have much time and would rather not waste it on Mack.

"And he was fine with that?"

"He said he had someone else he could go with. Look, I'd better get going. I'll see you tomorrow, okay?"

"Tilda, what's going on?"

"What do you mean?"

"I don't know. You just seem . . . like you're mad at me or something."

Tilda nodded her head slowly, squinting her eyes as if filtering Mack's words through them. "I hadn't thought of it that way," she said. She stood there and looked, all at once, full of disgust.

"I don't get it," Mack told her. "What did I do?"

"Nothing," she said. "That's what. You had me do your dirty work for you. You sat back and let me hurt somebody in the most ignoble"—it was a word from the college entrance exam—"way. You didn't have to hurt anyone. You got me to do it instead."

Mack stared at her. "You're the one who said you wanted to come with me. You're the one who was stupid enough to say yes to Carmine in the first place."

"What choice did I have? When you sit there and do nothing? Was *I* supposed to ask *you*? Why don't you do some of the work for once?" Tilda shook her head and walked away. She didn't speak to him for the next three days.

The day of the prom, Madame Lipsky took a final tally. She nodded with approval and told Mack, "I knew you'd do the right thing."

Mack tried to smile. He didn't dare look at Tilda, even though she had, twice that week, spoken to him briefly and even eaten lunch with him.

"And your friends?" Madame Lipsky asked the rest of the room. "They all set? Everyone's paired off?"

"Except for Carmine Bocchino," a girl called out. "I heard him in the cafeteria today. He said his date backed out and he can't find anyone."

Mack gave Tilda a covert glance. She looked surprised.

"Who was his date?" people were asking, but the girl said she didn't know.

"He didn't say her name." (He hadn't said any of the others, either, of course, but each of them had told someone.) "He just said he'd been stood up."

Madame Lipsky's face reddened and her mouth tensed. "This is unacceptable." She shook her head, bit her lip. "We can't stand back and let this happen."

Mack looked at the floor. He felt himself sweating. A crumpled note landed by his foot.

"HE TOLD ME HE HAD SOMEONE ELSE TO GO WITH!"

Prithi Desai raised her hand. "My little sister's never been to a prom before. She's a freshman. I'm sure she'd want to go."

"Where is she now?"

"Math, maybe? I'm not sure."

Madame Lipsky was scrawling something on a piece of notepaper. "Go to the office and find out. And find out where Carmine is. And when you've talked to her, go tell him."

The room filled with a sense of emergency. Since their class was seventh period—the last class of the day—Madame Lipsky wrote passes for the rest of the girls, too, so that they could go home and set their hair.

"Go, now, get going, make yourselves beautiful," she cried, shooing them out the door. The girls filed out of the room, even the ones who had never done anything with their hair and probably wouldn't tonight. Tilda collected her books and gave Mack a cold look. Glumly she told him, "See you at five."

Mack watched her and the other girls funnel into the hallway. With a piercing, explicit pang, he wondered if Tilda would ever truly like him again, the way she had liked him before.

In a few hours she would be by his side, in a magenta dress that tied in a halter behind her neck. She would dance with him, and with Geoff, and with Carmine Bocchino, whose date would spend most of the night with her sister instead. Carmine would go around with a fancy camera taking pictures of everyone, roll after roll, as if this were a wedding or some other occasion warranting an entire photo album. He would request a dance with each of the girls who had originally refused him, and they would each say yes, even Belle Gardner, since it was one thing to dance with him and another altogether to be his date for the night. They would dance. Across the country they were dancing—teens in ill-fitting tuxedos and strapless gowns, smiling for cameras, arms around each other, waiting for the flash. They had been dancing for months now, to "Twist and Shout" and "Pump the Jam" and "What I Like About You" and to songs they complained could not be danced to. Since April they had been ordering special creations from florists. All of May they had been doing fancy things with their hair. For the rest of June they would pile into limousines, drink cheap champagne, hold hands with people whose hands they didn't usually hold. In every state in the Union they would dance, had danced, were still dancing, in auditoriums and gyms laden with crepe streamers and balloons, in rented banquet rooms, and on fold-out dance floors. The dancing would continue for a few weeks more, and for years and years.

But for now it was still Fourth Year French, and the last girl had fluttered out the door. All that was left in the classroom was a bunch of eighteen-year-old boys and Madame Lipsky. She exhaled a sigh, smiling with relief. In her enormous plastic glasses and purple-tinted hair, she looked radiant. She had done what Mack had never done—and what he now longed, palpably, to be able to do. She had set all things right in the world.

Sunshine Cleaners

Any weekday in Brookline, drivers caught in Beacon Street traffic might see Sergei hurrying along a certain stretch of wet sidewalk. Sergei's back crooks slightly to the left, and his pants, baggy on thin, bowed legs, billow in the cold April air. If he's already completed his transaction, he'll be heading west, pockets sagging with quarters. When he arrives back at Sunshine Cleaners, he obeys the PUSH sign on the door, half expecting—one might call it hope—to find something changed. But there's old Lida behind the counter, smoking her second cigarette of the day, taking dirty silk shirts from a bald man. The man has also brought a pair of shoes to be resoled, and Lida is shaking her head.

"But the sign in the window says 'Shoe Repair,' " the man

protests. Other signs read, "24-Hour Tailoring," "Instant Zipper Fix," and "We Store Winter Furs!" but those are incorrect, too.

"Down the street," says Lida, already turning back to her sewing machine, while Sergei, now out of his snow-flecked red satin bomber jacket, begins work: taking piles of clothes around to the front, past the partition, into the laundry, over to the wall of bright yellow washing machines. All day he tosses clothes into washers and dryers and adds them to flat, folded stacks.

If it is a Monday, Sergei keeps an eye out for the tall girl. Last week she told him, "You disgust me!" This was after the change machine took her dollar without giving quarters, and Sergei, when notified, said, "Not my machine." Other customers have given up on Sergei—if they ever addressed him at all—and no longer bother to approach him when machines malfunction. Not the tall girl. When she offered him her other dollar for four quarters, Sergei just shook his head. That was when the tall girl yelled, "You disgust me!" The two other customers looked frightened, not realizing that Sergei and the tall girl have such conversations regularly. Sometimes Lida, from her wooden seat in front of the Singer, joins in while hemming a skirt, not looking up, yelling, "*You* disgust *me!*" or "Not *my* machine!" or something in Russian that the tall girl can't understand.

The tall girl always does her wash on Mondays, when there are fewer people. Strong, fit, with blond hair that meets her shoulders, and clear, flawless skin, she looks to be in her early twenties. If a dryer doesn't work and Sergei tells her, "Not my machine," she confronts him with frank eyes that at times force Sergei to look to the ground. She speaks in the flat voice of someone used to having her demands met. After firing some comment at Sergei, she transfers her clothes to another dryer, then sits and reads. Usually she peruses magazines, but last week it was a book, *Love: Ten Poems by Pablo Neruda*, from which she copied phrases, every few minutes or so, onto a sheet of paper.

Her easy confidence Sergei sees as purely American. When the dryer buzzes, she sweeps out her clean clothes heedlessly, a clumsy shower of mixed cotton; she does not separate dark and light loads. Sergei has never seen her give any article of clothing special treatment, to be air-dried or placed flat. Her clothes are mostly denim and jersey, solid colors. She has no fancy fabrics or patterned socks like the other girls doing their laundry. But her underpants, Sergei has noticed, are the satin kind with just a thin band down the back.

Today, though, is a Thursday. It might as well be Tuesday, Wednesday, or Friday. Lida has turned the radio to Easy Jazz 107.9, filling the air with the thin, slinky whine of an electronic alto sax. Outside, Beacon Street is already busy with altercations, a wrangle of horns. It has been a long winter, and even the cars are starting to show it—rusty, tired, snapping at each other. The snow began in early December and doesn't seem to have finished. Down the street, store windows display flowered dresses, straw Easter bonnets, pastel pocketbooks.

Inside Sunshine Cleaners, the morning bustle is fluorescent-lit and smoky. People drop off broken computers; Sergei's friend Val runs a computer repair business and tells perplexed early-risers to leave their machines at the cleaners. Sergei wonders about Val, a widower a good twenty years older than Sergei. Val has been in this country longer, nine years. It was Val who stood in wool pants and bright red suspenders to meet Sergei at the airport two years ago, holding a sign with his name on it. All they had in common was a mutual Moscow acquaintance with whom neither has kept in touch. Now Val and Sergei play poker with two other men every Friday. The men are not yet sixty but look ancient—teeth missing, hair gone. Their skin is gray-green and deeply wrinkled. They tease Sergei because he is slim-boned and lean, and call him "Omar" because of his dark coloring and high cheekbones.

From its wide spout, the fabric softener pours a lazy pink veil. At cards last week Sergei lost four days' pay. Val sat across from him in a peaked flannel cap, winning, smoking ceaselessly, complaining of frequent doctors' visits for lung tests. This computer business of his has to be a sham. How could a fifty-year-old from Smolensk, rotted through with emphysema, know a thing about computers? Val claims never to have touched one until he came to America, says one day he just found one, took it apart, and figured out how it worked. "It's just a little chip!" he has said. He claims to know all the programs, all the languages, and tells Sergei, when asked how he does it, "I'm a genius!"

Sergei adds bleach to a load of whites. Nearby, Mr. Tyne, the young freckled man who owns the washers and dryers, is making his daily visit to empty them of their quarters. He says nothing.

Sergei wonders when he'll next have luck at cards. Ivan, the eldest, gambles on anything—horses, dogs, Val's test results. He plays the Massachusetts lottery regularly, claims to know someone who won. He and his wife have been here three years. "On the T today," Ivan said recently, "I saw a man with a mole out to here!" He held his gray-green hand an inch from his chin and shivered with disapproval. "I come all the way to America, I'd like to not see such a thing, *for once in my life.*" That last bit is in English, one of the few American phrases Ivan uses (often, and somewhat indiscriminately).

Sergei thinks of his own skewed back. Ivan must disapprove; his wife is a big old St. Petersburg beauty with perfectly sculpted hair and eyebrows. On poker nights she puts on dark lipstick, tan stockings, and matching outfits from twenty years ago to go see a movie with her friends. Her ankles puff over the tops of little fur-lined boots.

The change machine is broken again, but Mr. Tyne has already left, his bag heavy with loot. Sergei hopes Val won't raise the stakes again this Friday. The third man is a retired physicist named Miro. He has bad luck with poker and mutters to himself in Belorussian. His wife does things in the kitchen all night long, and every half-hour or so calls out some comment or other, always something brief, anxious, and inconsequential.

When Sergei sits in Miro's dark apartment on a Friday night, dealing out the worn plastic cards, he thinks to himself that all over this city young people must be having fun and making love. For some reason—the long hours at Sunshine Cleaners, he supposes—he has yet to find those people. American ones, that is. Not the Russians Val has introduced him to, and whom he sees frequently: glossy-haired Yelena, her sister; her cousin; their neighbors and friends. He's in America now; why should he hang around with them all the time? When he walks home from work at seven every evening, Sergei wishes there were a bar to stop into on the way, where he could meet other thirty-year-olds. People outside of his circle, friends to make on his own, nothing to do with Yelena. But it's a college town founded by Puritans; the only bar on his route is a big one with booths and fried food and students in baseball caps.

Sergei wonders about the tall girl, what she does when she

isn't reading magazines or copying poetry or telling Sergei, "You disgust me!" Perhaps her friends, like Sergei's, are aging geniuses. Sergei doubts it. He pictures them young and female. He has run out of quarters.

He will have to run down the block to change a twenty. Lida has gone on her lunch break, so there is no one to leave in charge; on a piece of paper Sergei scrawls "Back in 5 Minutes" and tapes it to the glass door, which he locks behind him. He hurries to the nearby liquor store. There is rarely a line there, at most someone asking for the on-sale cigarettes or buying a lottery ticket.

It happened once that he hurried back, nearly out of breath, to find the tall girl scowling in front of the door, her hands on her curved hips, and a plastic bin of dirty clothes in front of her. "People have lives to get to," she said in that firm voice of hers. "People don't have all day."

"Neither do I," said Sergei.

"You have time to run to the liquor store," the girl said. Her hair was pulled back in a clip, so that her skin looked especially luminous. "I see where you go. Don't bother denying it. And meanwhile your customers have to wait."

Sergei felt his face heat up. Why didn't he say anything then? Why did he just unlock the latch and, feeling his heart pounding, walk ahead of the tall girl without holding the door? From inside Sunshine Cleaners he watched her bend down to lift her laundry, and, without even trying, saw right up her denim skirt. He pretended not to notice as she struggled with the bin of clothes and an unwieldy bottle of detergent. Afterward, he had a horrible headache.

Sergei replays this in his mind as he enters the liquor store. The manager recognizes Sergei, knows why he's here, greets him in a not-unfriendly manner. Sergei hands over a bill and takes back coins. How many times have their hands touched this way? Sergei leaves the store, passing shivering trees and an enigmatic sign announcing APRIL 25: HAZARDOUS WASTE DAY! He takes up his restrained run, his back at a tilt, pants parachuting. He considers that people may be watching him.

He does not understand that his red satin bomber jacket looks like a remnant of high school varsity and is insufficient for a New England winter. He does not realize that people who come to Sunshine Cleaners suppose he is Lida's son, or that they suspect he is slightly ill—a Chernobyl victim, perhaps?—with his sunken cheeks and tweaked body.

He does not know that last week the tall girl called the Chamber of Commerce to complain about him, or that the woman on the phone told the girl, in a bright Brahmin accent, that Sunshine Cleaners was not a member of the Brookline Chamber, so that the girl now pictures the Chamber of Commerce as some sort of blue-haired ladies' club. The girl was given a telephone number that turned out to belong to the Consumer Complaint Bureau, where a different woman asked, with a harsh South Boston inflection, "Have you lost any money?"

"Well, yeah, some quarters, a few dollars, I guess. But it's not the money; it's the rudeness, I mean—"

"I can only lodge a complaint if money has been lost. If you don't like the way they run their business, there's nothing we can do except urge you to take your business elsewhere."

These are just some of the things that Sergei does not know.

. . .

Today is Tuesday. Wednesday? Sergei shuffle-runs down the street. He arrives at Sunshine Cleaners, takes a breath, pushes the door that says "PUSH." What change could he possibly expect to find inside? That Lida will be suddenly young and unwrinkled, like a replumped raisin? That her hair will be blond, her figure slim, and she will look at him when she speaks? Instead he smells cigarette smoke, sees the same faces, the broken machines.

Last night he had dinner with Yelena and her younger sister, Sonia. They ate hamburgers downtown, and Sergei admired Sonia, who had dyed her hair blue-black and pierced her eyebrow with a small silver hoop. Yelena said it was horrible, but Sergei could only like Sonia for it. Amazing what difference a few years can make; Yelena still spoke with an accent and wore embarrassing lace-up shoes, while Sonia, five years younger, looked and sounded American and had a skateboarding boyfriend named Timothy. Timothy met them after dinner, and the couple went off together.

Sergei wonders where they went. He wonders if the girls' cousin Johnny (he gave himself that name) knows of any good parties going on this coming weekend. Johnny doesn't always invite Sergei along, only when he happens to see him right beforehand.

Sergei works his way across the wall of yellow washers and dryers. Around ten, Val shows up to claim a computer keyboard. He flirts with Lida for a bit before telling Sergei, "Ivan wants to go to Foxwoods next Friday."

"The casino?"

"In Connecticut. Ivan says he knows someone who won big."

Sergei heads to the other side of the partition to start a new load.

"Where's your enthusiasm, Omar?" Val calls to him. "It could be fun."

"What do people play?" Sergei calls back. "Poker?"

"Everything! Blackjack! Slot machines!"

"No machines," says Sergei. "I'm sick of machines."

"We can all four play together," Val says through his cloud of cigarette smoke. "You might win. Right? You could win something. Anything could happen!"

"Next Friday, then?"

"Unless my doctor's appointment goes late. I've got another evaluation that afternoon."

"Everything all right?"

"Of course not. You of all people, asking me that, with that spine of yours." Val picks up the broken keyboard. "Your back, my heart, we're all breaking down. All these breakdowns!" He winks at Lida and heads for the door. "Till tomorrow!"

Sergei checks the pockets of a pair of baggy pants before adding them to the cycle. He finds a roll of breath mints. They have the same scent as a mint that an aunt who raised him sometimes gave him when he behaved. He shuts his eyes to find the memory, but Lida says, "What does it mean, 'Hazardous Waste Day'? How could they celebrate a thing like that?"

"It's not a festival."

"I wouldn't be surprised, in this town. It's always something: flag day, flu vaccination day, cat-spaying day, voting day.

That must be what it is: checking for toxic garbage. I like this town. They make sure everything is okay."

Today is Monday. Sergei stands in Sunshine Cleaners with a cart full of laundry. The tall girl is glowering at him.

A washer has left her clothes in a sudsy bath instead of rinsed clean. Sergei has again told her, "Not my machine," but she refuses to budge. So Sergei adds, "Tell the owners," and points to the telephone number inscribed on a small sign on the wall.

The girl takes a slow breath. "Fine, then, I'm going to call them." She heads toward the phone on Lida's counter.

"This is our phone," Sergei tells her, blocking her way with his body. "Not theirs. The laundry is a separate business."

The girl raises her hand in an ambiguous half-fist: she could be about to punch him, or she could be about to pull out her own hair. "Then may I use your phone?" she asks, her jaw tightening visibly.

Sergei pauses for a thoughtful moment before saying, "No."

The tall girl looks him in the eye, pushes past him to the counter, and picks up the phone. She dials a number and says angry things to an answering machine. Sergei watches the way her blond hair falls pleasingly forward across her face.

"This is pitiful," she says when she hangs up. "This is no way to run a business. You're rude, and your machines never work. My clothes come back smelling of cigarettes."

"So don't come here," Sergei says, knowing at once that he

does not mean it. Except for Val's visits, would Sergei even exist here, without the tall girl to notice him?

"This is the only laundry nearby. I don't have a car. How can you treat me this way?" The girl has begun crying; this has never happened before.

"So you don't have a car," Lida says from the other side of the room, threading a bobbin on the Singer. "I waited three years for a car. When it came, it was orange and made of plastic. I had to pick it up in Petrozavodsk. I broke the door just getting in to drive it home." This is all in Russian, so the tall girl does not reply.

"I need quarters, too," Sergei is saying. "The owner doesn't give me a discount. When he comes to take the money from the machines, he doesn't even talk to me. Do you know how that makes me—? I use the machines just like you."

"Well, then, we're all pathetic," the girl says through tears.

Sergei hasn't stopped talking. "I have to run to the liquor store to change my dollars. If Lida's not here, I have to lock the door; I have to hurry, and it hurts my back. I have a bad spine, I take quinine at night. I didn't use to be this way. I was strong, but one day . . ." Sergei hears his voice crack. That's it. He feels those tears, ready to reveal themselves the minute he blinks. He stops talking and concentrates on not blinking, tries to distract himself by focusing on one of Val's broken-down computer monitors. The tall girl, without appearing to have heard him, has begun sobbing.

"Same with the telephone," Lida is saying, as the sewing machine hums along efficiently. "We lived in that apartment two years before they gave us our phone. Then it didn't ring. We could only make outgoing calls. People thought we were never home."

But Sergei, suddenly exhausted, is not listening, and the tall girl has already gone to the other side of the partition, to sit on a plastic chair and cry.

Today is Friday. Sergei runs to the liquor store for quarters. He's thinking about the piece of paper in his pocket. He won't look at it again yet. Not that he hasn't already memorized the lines, even looked up one of the words in his English-Russian dictionary. He'll wait until he has finished one more load, and then he'll allow himself another glance at the loopy blue handwriting. But first, the quarters. It's cold inside the liquor store. An unclean man in front of Sergei is buying something called the "Mega Millions."

"One hundred and forty-two million," the manager says. "I bought my ticket, alright." He is already opening a roll of quarters for Sergei when Sergei tells him, "I will buy a ticket."

The manager hands Sergei a long card on which there are many numbered boxes. Sergei looks at it and is overwhelmed. With the manager's pen, he fills in a few of the boxes. He is sure he ought to be choosing his numbers more carefully but worries he is taking too much time. He does not realize that he has used only part of his card, that there are more numbers to choose from.

He turns his card in incomplete and shuffle-runs back to Sunshine Cleaners, ticket in hand, past the sign announcing HAZARDOUS WASTE DAY! On the trees that line the sidewalk, tiny retracted buds shrink back from the cold. Rich? Who said Sergei wanted to be rich? It's a vague term, and Sergei wants concrete things: An entertainment center with surround sound. A Honda motorcycle. A pair of Ray Ban sunglasses. He would like to go to California at some point.

Val comes by at ten. "There may be some drop-offs this afternoon," he tells Sergei. "I have a doctor's appointment."

Lida looks up from her sewing machine.

"More tests, huh?" says Sergei.

"More tests. We decided to postpone Foxwoods." Val's fingertips are yellow with nicotine.

"I bought a lottery ticket," Sergei tells him. "One hundred and forty-two million."

Val slaps him with approval and says, "Ivan knows someone who won."

"Yeah, yeah."

"You never know," Val says. "Anything could happen!"

It's true. Like Monday, after the tall girl finished crying and stood up abruptly to gather her clothes, and a scrap of paper fell out of her magazine. Sergei just watched it land on the linoleum floor beside the plastic chair. It was still there after the girl left. When Sergei got home that night, he looked up the word "abyss."

Now, as he heads around to the front counter, he notices the way Val and Lida are speaking to each other. Why isn't she looking at her sewing machine? Sergei finds himself wondering. Val touches her shoulder while saying something, and Lida's eyelids drop slightly.

"I lie in this cold abyss," Sergei thinks to himself. That's what the scrap of paper said. Well, actually, that part was crossed out. But Sergei looked hard to figure out what was hidden underneath the scratches. After that part, he read:

The goodbye of your eyes
to me in the cold bed abyss
Weeks emptied of you
are mountains harsh and steep
Like a flower I wilt
without your

That was how it ended, as if falling off a cliff. Now, Sergei notes, Val is lightly touching Lida's elbow. She says something to him about her two tabby cats, and Val, coughing, says he would like to meet them.

Sergei doesn't like to remember things. It's a superstition of his. Pleasant memories—being with friends at age thirteen and laughing so hard their guts ached, or eating Turkish figs with a girl in the park in June—such memories leap past him quickly, and Sergei cannot focus enough to make the moments linger. But when the bad memories seep back, like they always do, they stick, so vivid that Sergei finds himself frightened. He is frightened that he won't be able to get out, that he'll blink and find himself back in some long-gone moment: shivering in front of a broken space-heater; lying on a Moscow street in a pool of his own blood, hearing someone say, "Careful with his neck."

When this happens, Sergei shakes himself, like a dog just out of a lake. He really would not be surprised if one day such a memory, so real—the smell of the bloody pavement, of the stranger's damp shoes, the sound of a woman's voice saying, "Is he alive? Don't move him"—forced him back to that midnight street, and he had to go through it all again.

He would like to reverse this somehow, make the good memories stick, or to produce kinder images so strong that they might actually occur. He wants to do this but cannot. Maybe that's why he was put off by Val's bit of abracadabra this past Friday.

Val brought a computer to poker. He pushed the chips and card deck aside and slid a small monitor onto Miro's table. He connected wires and even the telephone line and dialed a number. "You said you missed Petersburg!" he said happily and slapped Ivan on the shoulder. "Well, take a look here!"

Sergei stood beside Val, with Ivan and Miro looking over his shoulder. He had never seen such bright colors on a computer screen. The ones in the laundry were never on. This one had a turquoise pattern, with text in various hues. Val typed things, and the telephone rang in a muted way. "Wait until you see this."

A photograph emerged on the screen. There was a building of some sort, with people in front. Sergei was amazed by the clarity. But it wasn't a photograph, it moved. "Look familiar?" Val asked, turning to Ivan.

"I can't believe it. The university library."

"Live coverage. Some students have put a camera lens facing it. Anybody who goes in is on film. It's for research or something. What do you think of that!"

"Miraculous!" said Miro, and Ivan said softly, "It's like I'm right back there. *For once in my life.*"

"It's on twenty-four hours," Val explained. "The wonders of the Internet." He smiled at Sergei and said, "Not bad, eh, Omar?"

But to Sergei this seemed somehow unfair. This satellite image, or whatever it was, it was too real. Like bad memories.

They shouldn't be able to look back at something like this, so simple and nice, and far away, so easily.

Why can't good memories be easy like this? Sergei would like to be like Val and turn pleasant daydreams into concrete visions. When he confronts the glass-and-metal door with the "PUSH" sign every morning, he tries to imagine something other than what's there, certain that if he thinks hard enough of what he wants to be inside, it just might happen.

Luckily, Sergei ran into Yelena's cousin Johnny this past Saturday. Johnny is an audio technician whom the women all seem to like, and he took Sergei along to a party hosted by two Americans he works with. This was in Dorchester, with lots of beer.

A woman from Waltham paid attention to Sergei. She asked him about his back, and he told her about being mugged and left for dead.

"A couple coming home from a disco found me," he explained. "Saved my life, probably. I was in hospital six months."

To show that she understood what Sergei had gone through, the woman told him, "My brother-in-law fell off a roof and landed on a metal rake. He almost died. If he had landed one millimeter to the left, the rake could have gone through his heart. He's okay now, though. You never know what's gonna happen."

Sergei tried to picture the man, the roof, the confusingly placed metal rake, and could make no sense of the logistics. But he took the woman's phone number and has considered calling her sometime this week. There is a movie about female vampires he wouldn't mind seeing. That's how it happens, Sergei knows.

You call and make your offer—a movie, a drink, maybe dinner. It happens all the time, all over, especially in spring. He is sure of that now. This morning he saw Lida standing close to Val, talking about potatoes, of all things, saying she knew a recipe that he was sure to like. Val's skin was no longer so green but instead almost rosy.

Well, Val's heart may be getting better, but seeing him smiling there Sergei felt a cold spot in his own. Why can't he have that? No, not Lida. Maybe with Sheri from Waltham. At any rate, it's too soon to call, only Monday. Outside, the air is cold for April, but the tree buds aren't yet dead, just knotted up patiently on their branches. At Sunshine Cleaners, the tall girl is standing in front of Sergei, announcing that the change machine is broken again. "Not my machine," says Sergei.

"Well, I think you should at least write 'Out of Order' on it, so that other people don't lose money trying to use it."

"There's a light," says Sergei, meaning the little orange one that lights up next to the words "Out of Order."

"The light's not on."

"Then it's working."

But the girl won't move. "No, it's not working."

"Yes, it is," says Sergei. "See?" He walks up to the machine, takes a dollar from his pocket, and slides it into the machine's thin mouth. He and the tall girl watch as the dollar is sucked in, and for a few seconds nothing happens.

But then the quarters begin to pour out, first into the little cup below the machine, and then onto the floor. The quarters keep coming, hundreds of them clinking out and landing in a noisy pile. Sergei and the tall girl watch together, for minutes, it seems, until the machine's bowels have been emptied.

Calamity

On the floor, the shiny pile barely resembles coins. Sergei and the tall girl just look at it for a moment. Then the girl bends down and picks up four quarters, and Sergei sees where the band of her underwear meets her skin.

When she walks back over to her dirty clothes, Sergei goes to the other side of the partition and returns with a medium-sized plastic bag, into which he begins scooping the coins. He knows the tall girl is watching. He ignores her as she waits there with her paperback, whose cover says *A Woman Scorned*. When he has filled the bag with all of the quarters, Sergei brings it to the other side of the partition.

After about twenty minutes, the tall girl transfers her clothes to a big yellow dryer and then sits down to read again. That is when Mr. Tyne makes his daily visit and, without saying hello to Sergei or Lida, begins his rounds, emptying the quarters from washers and dryers, one by one. After fifteen minutes or so, he progresses to the change machine, opening it up to take the dollars. He removes the bills, counts them up, and then says to Sergei, "Hey, you have any idea what's going on with this machine?"

Sergei shakes his head.

"All the quarters are gone, but there's only forty-two bucks here. I've never seen the machine empty before. You notice anything odd about it?"

"Not my machine," says Sergei.

He sees the tall girl staring at him over her book, her hair pulled back from her rosy skin. Mr. Tyne collects his money, refills the machine with quarters, and prepares to leave. He pulls the door open and exits.

Sergei looks over at the tall girl, though he is tired and wants no more trouble; their fights can be exhausting. But he dares to look at her. Their eyes lock, her stare expectant, and Sergei thinks—with surprise, for some reason—"She despises me."

Now that he has allowed himself to think this, Sergei cannot stand it. He must apologize to her. Not for his own behavior, which he knows will not change, and not for having taken the scrap of paper, which she'll never know, but for whatever it is that has made her so sullen, whatever caused her to sit on the plastic chair that day and cry.

Or perhaps it was Sergei, just Sergei and nothing else, that made her cry. After all, he disgusts her.

He wishes he had not taken the money, knows that that, too, must disgust her. There must be something he can do about it, prove that he is not so disgusting. He thinks of what he can tell her, that in fact he is donating the money to the town Police Department, or to the Committee for the Elderly. Anything to stop this. How many times have they yelled cruel things back and forth? He is tired of hurting, his back and his feelings. All that incivility, what a waste of energy. That's it: he will say that the money is going to the Hazardous Waste Board.

He takes a breath and says, "About that money."

The tall girl says, "You hit the jackpot there, didn't you?" This must suddenly strike her as funny. Like a rainbow or some other naturally occurring wonder, apparently shocking the girl as much as Sergei, a surprised smile breaks across her face.

"Hit the jackpot," Sergei repeats. "That's good. I guess I did. Something good. For once in my life."

"Or maybe twice in a life," says the girl, tilting her head slightly. "I'd like to think it's at least twice."

The Man from Allston Electric

Rhea couldn't help but feel sorry for the man from Allston Electric. He had fiddled all afternoon at an electrical outlet in her drafty living room only to emerge rumpled and disappointed, muttering, "Can't do it." He found Rhea in the kitchen, where the fluorescent light turned him gray under the eyes. "Nope. Wire's dead." Though he said this definitively, it was clear from his tense jaw that what the man wanted more than anything at that moment was to be able to revive the wire and impress Rhea.

Sitting at the nicked kitchen table, which she'd turned into a computer desk for the day, Rhea felt a small rush of pleasure. She was grateful for any admission of failure. She was tired of everyone always saying, Of course it can be done, Rhea, of course your love life can be renewed, your career saved. All around her the facts screamed: No! Yet even her closest friends at first remained hopeful after learning that Gregory had moved out. Though they saw for themselves that his dented Civic was no longer accruing tickets at the curb outside, and that Rhea no longer wore the little green-beaded bracelet he'd given her, they passed along books with titles like *When Love Isn't Enough* and spelled out names of therapists who had saved various relationships—or at least prolonged them for months, sometimes years. Rhea's mother, meanwhile, insisted that Rhea would find someone better, as if Gregory were a vacuum cleaner that had stopped working.

Rhea never allowed herself to say to her, What if *nothing* gets better? She woke up every morning at seven o'clock in the pale yellow bedroom she had once shared with Gregory, and wished for good news. It wasn't a conscious wish, more like a vague hope that was there when she awoke and gradually diminished as the day waned. Mornings seemed to hold possibilities, the way the light shone in through the little window across from the bed, tattooing slant rectangles on the wall where Gregory's desk had been. His chess magazines, Rhea realized months after he moved out, still sat in a little pile in the corner. One day Rhea would bring them downstairs to the recycling bin; she knew this. But she also knew that she could not do it yet, though the magazine pile was gauzy with dust.

The living room, on the other hand, no longer showed any sign of having been inhabited by anyone other than Rhea. Her fiberboard bookshelves and filing cabinets cluttered the side of the room ruled by her large oak desk. Atop one of the shelves, tucked in an oversized manila envelope, was the wad of dissertation—on apostrophe in the Petrarchan sonnet—that she had completed a year earlier. Though it had won her much praise in her department, no one seemed to want to publish it. The library had a typed copy that no one would ever read. Rhea had received numerous direct-mail offers to have her work bound in book form, with an engraved leather cover. The mailings kept coming, like those twelve-CDs-for-a-dollar music clubs.

Each day Rhea sat in front of her hand-me-down computer writing job applications, query letters, and proposals for post-doctoral fellowships, all the while listening to the classic rock station on the radio. When advertisements came on, she grimaced at the mottoes of the world: *Be all that you can be! Just do it!*

For this reason it was a relief to see the man from Allston Electric standing in her kitchen doorway, his worker's hands shoved shamefully into the pockets of acid-washed jeans, explaining that he couldn't do it, that no one could, that the power line was broken somewhere behind the wall, irreparable. "Problem with these prewar buildings," he went on. "I can see they haven't kept this one up too good."

Rhea nodded and took a bite from a ripe pear. She was constantly hungry. She had, for the past year, been snacking nearly every hour (bananas, peanuts, Swiss chocolates on sale that week) and felt heavy with extra pounds, though she hadn't actually gained weight. In fact she was skinny, as she always had been. It had crossed her mind at one point that perhaps she had a worm of some sort, but she knew deep down that this wasn't so, and that it would, like everything else in life, pass. She looked at the man, of whom she had been only vaguely aware since telling him, two hours earlier, the whole little story, complete with sound effects, about the lamp she had turned on, and the hissing noise, and how she used that outlet all the time, since it was the only other one where she could plug in her computer, which had a cord with three prongs, and on which she was revising her doctoral dissertation.

The man from Allston Electric had looked straight into her eyes as he listened, frowning at appropriate moments. He then lowered his chin to his chest and said gravely, "We can't have this interrupting your career."

He had approached the outlet with vigilance. But now he looked let down—let down like no repairman Rhea had ever seen. The old building was in poor shape; for the consequent affordability Gregory had selected it, and for this reason Rhea was able to continue renting the apartment alone now that Gregory was gone. The landlord hadn't visited the place in years, and appliances were often keeling over in melodramatic ways. One day the oven spontaneously caught fire; a sudden flame like a blowtorch scorched a loaf of zucchini bread Rhea was baking. When the smoke subsided, Rhea saw that an entire section of the oven was nothing but ash. In the "Description" column of the receipt the next day, a repairman scrawled "exploding oven" as if it were a common occurrence.

Always men came to fix these problems, and looked pleased when Rhea—with her dark hair and wide-set, if slightly uneven, eyes—answered the door. The man from Allston Electric hadn't even swaggered into the apartment the way the men usually did, winking and wielding tools. He had knocked lightly on the door, twice, with a slight pause in between. When Rhea opened the door, he was holding a battered black toolbox, perfectly still, with his feet apart in a way that made him look like someone had told him not to move. He said, "Allston Electric," and followed

Rhea to the living room. There he had worked conscientiously, quietly. But it hadn't paid off; the line was still dead.

"I came with a Band-Aid, and what you need is open-heart surgery, you see what I'm saying?" he told her now. "Replacing the dead wire, that'll mean knocking out the whole wall."

"But I need to be able to use that outlet." Pear juice was dribbling down her wrist, and Rhea felt, if only for a moment, utterly discomposed.

"The best I can do for now is tie up the dead wire and connect the existing line to the busted outlet. I just gotta call my boss now, though. To let him know that it's surgery, not a Band-Aid. Mind if I use your phone? He always has me check in."

The man from Allston Electric held the phone to his ear a few moments before someone picked up. Rhea watched him speak into the receiver. He was slight and freckled, in his late twenties like her, Rhea guessed. As he spoke to his boss, the muscles in his jaw tensed. "Swear to God," he was saying, "I checked everything. Line's dead, man, I swear."

There was something almost handsome about him, Rhea decided, but in a way that more than anything proved the great distance between "almost" and "handsome." A perfectly nice nose, but too big for the fine-boned face. Rhea watched the man's lips move and noted that although he had a nicely dimpled jaw, his mouth was small in relation. She felt inexplicably saddened, watching this face with its various pleasant features. They were features that must have once seemed to hold much promise, but that he had somehow never grown into. Probably, Rhea concluded, people had told him when he was a child that he was good-looking, and now he was spending the rest of his life realizing that it wasn't necessarily true.

"He wants to see for himself," he told Rhea when he put down the receiver. "He's coming here—Mike, my boss. He wants to make sure." The man bit at the corner of his lip. "It's like he doesn't believe me."

"I'm sure you did everything right," Rhea said, though she had no reason to think that, really. To demonstrate her reasoning, she added, "You were in there a very long time."

"Yeah, thanks," the man said. "I don't know why Mike doesn't trust me. He gets that way sometimes. But I don't say anything about it. Mike, he's my fiancée's brother. I don't want to cause any problems in the family, see."

"When are you getting married?"

"Two months. We've been together two years. Lucky for me. My mother was really starting to harp on me, and then Laura, she was, too, talking about her biological clock, you know."

Rhea nodded. She had recently turned twenty-eight and was certain that she wouldn't fall in love with anyone in time to create a baby.

"Well, yeah, so there was some pressure to, you know, tie the knot."

Rhea was going to tie the knot with Gregory, and then one night three months before the wedding, when they were driving home from a late movie, Gregory pulled his car over just off Storrow Drive, put on the parking brake, and said in a frightened voice, "I can't do this." Rhea thought she would probably wonder for the rest of her life if throughout the entire movie he had been worrying about what he was going to say to her.

It had now been over a year since Gregory had left, over a year since Rhea had felt a man's bare arms around her. Over a year since she had felt the sureness of sitting next to Gregory at a party or in a restaurant and knowing that afterward, without awkwardness, they would go home and get into the big, messy bed and make love. In the morning she used to wake up and, always, find him already awake, composing ideal mates on a miniature magnetic chessboard. Even if she didn't move, just opened her eyes, he would always notice the moment she awoke, reach over and clumsily brush his palm along the side of her head.

Now there were just men. Rhea had gone on dates with a number of them in the past ten months, at first with something close to enthusiasm, and later with something more like dread. The last date she had agreed to was weeks ago, a friend from an internship back in grad school. He took her to a South End restaurant, and when they finished eating, Rhea checked the time and said with surprise, "It's later than I thought."

"What time is it?" the man had asked, and then reached over and turned Rhea's wrist toward him to glance at her watch. Afterward, in her mind, Rhea saw this action over and over again, this perfectly nice young man reaching over before she could realize it, taking her wrist in his hand, and each time she disliked him even more, until she knew that she never wanted to see him again.

There was another man, too, whose phone calls Rhea wasn't returning. He was a good seven years younger and ended his telephone messages by saying, "Later." He wrote little e-mails titled "Howdie!" and "Chow!"

The one she liked was the one it could never work out with. He was the former boyfriend of her best childhood friend, so that even now that he was single there was no chance of a future with him.

Rhea hadn't had sex in over a year. It struck her as phenomenal that she had survived, that people all around her were somehow surviving alone in single beds. Not so much without sex; what surprised Rhea was the fact that she had gone for over a year without feeling her hand in another warm hand, or her arm about another's waist, had not leaned over to quickly kiss Gregory on the cheek, just a momentary, automatic, almost involuntary action. That unwanted hand on her wrist at the restaurant was nothing like Gregory's easy, relaxed hand on her thigh, or her neck, or her shoulder, which had known it had a right to be there.

Rhea hadn't felt anything like that in more than a year. There were moments when such thoughts were enough to stop her mid-motion. She would find herself staring at the kitchen cabinet, reaching up for a bottle of vitamins, and then realize that her arm was sore: how long had she been standing there like that?

The man from Allston Electric was leaning on the Formica counter. "Mike said he'd come here as soon as he could, but I don't know how soon. I'm really sorry about this. Man, I hope he doesn't find some way to fix it that I didn't see."

"What if he does?" Rhea asked. "Can he punish you?" She didn't mean for this to sound menacing, but it came out that way. The man from Allston Electric stood up straight and raised his eyebrows.

"Well, he can't fire me, since he's Laura's brother. What he'll do is, he'll tell Laura, and then Laura'll say, when I get home tonight, 'Mikey says you screwed up big-time at work today,' and then she'll look at me like this and wait for me to explain myself.

Like she wants me to prove that I'm worth marrying. And I'll have to say something smart back. To reassure her."

Never had a repairman been so forthcoming, Rhea reflected. But the man continued.

"One time Mike clipped the wrong wire, and I caught it. Sort of saved the day. And I told Laura, and she looked so relieved, like it was all she wanted to hear. Like she'd had doubts about me, you know?"

"My ex was like that," Rhea said, surprising herself. "I think he needed constant proof that he'd made the right decision in falling in love with me. I remember one day I complained about a professor of mine. I thought that Gregory would comfort me. He just gave me this look, as if maybe the whole time he'd been wrong to think that I was intelligent."

"I know that look," said the man from Allston Electric.

"I could tell what he was thinking," Rhea continued. "That maybe I was just some mediocre student. And the thing is, that made me start to wonder if maybe I really was mediocre. And that made me start to doubt Gregory himself: because why was he with me, if I was mediocre?" Rhea remembered what had happened next. How, if only momentarily, their entire relationship had seemed to her nothing more than a union of two unworthy souls, a mistake that could be snuffed out with the tip of a finger. But Rhea had never acknowledged to Gregory this pattern of thought, and so they had never spoken about it.

She supposed that Gregory had had no such doubts about Jeannine Piolat. He had met her while in Paris for a conference on Contemporary Phenomenology. This he told Rhea that same night after the movie, as the Honda deposited exhaust at the side of the road. No, Jeannine was not a philosopher or an academic. She was a dancer in an avant-garde troupe whose performance he just happened to have seen. Rhea imagined a long-haired woman with a translucent scarf around her neck.

Rhea tried to halt her thoughts. "Where's the wedding going to be?" she asked the man.

"Mike's wife's parents' house. They have a big yard. Out in Woburn. Listen, I'm really sorry about the wait. But when Mike's doing other stuff—well, he takes his time."

"It's okay."

The man held out his right hand and breathed in. "I'm Lonny." He pronounced it "Lowonny." Then, sounding as if he were asking Rhea to a dance, he added, "Mind if I ask your name?" Rhea shook his hand and told him.

"Rhea," he repeated. "That's pretty. Does it mean something?"

"It's from Greek mythology," she said, but didn't bother explaining. No one had ever called her name "pretty" before.

"My name just means Lonny. It's not even short for anything." He looked at her for a few seconds, and Rhea looked back at her computer screen, pretending not to notice that he was watching her. She felt a sudden craving for potato chips. "You alright working in here?" Lonny asked. "There's barely any light."

He was right. Rhea had moved her computer to the kitchen for the afternoon sun, but hours had passed, and the sky outside was now a dim winter pink. "I'm just staring at a computer screen anyway," Rhea said. Lonny looked concerned that he had said something wrong, so that Rhea heard herself adding, "But you're right, it's pretty gloomy in here." The walls, once off-white, had aged into a dirty yellow, and the cabinets were of a cheap dark brown wood. The fluorescent light tinged the room sallow. One of the overhead bulbs had burned out some time since Gregory left, and even standing on a chair Rhea couldn't reach it.

She looked at Lonny and felt she should do something. "Would you like something to eat?" was what she came up with.

"Oh, no, that's okay, thanks," Lonny said bashfully. But Rhea felt certain Lonny was as hungry as she was. She stood and took a box of oatmeal cookies from a cabinet, saying, "Here's a snack, if you'd like." Then, without asking, she took a cookie out of the box, handed it to Lonny, and said, "It doesn't really matter what Mike finds." She had wanted this to be uplifting, but her voice, she decided, made it sound nihilistic.

Lonny said, "Thanks, thanks very much," and immediately began to eat. Back in front of her computer, pretending not to see Lonny anymore, Rhea ate, too.

And then she found herself speaking. She didn't look away from her computer screen. "I know you're right," she told him. "I'm sure of it."

Why was she so sure, she immediately wondered. She must have just said it to make the man feel better. Without shifting her gaze, she could see Lonny stop chewing. He looked at her with wide eyes. "I appreciate it," he said, almost in a whisper. And then he raised his voice a notch and said, "I'd better leave you to your work."

Lonny went into the open hallway that connected the kitchen to the little sitting room and sat on the tweed loveseat Rhea had bought at the Salvation Army. His right leg began to jiggle nervously. Rhea could see this out of the corner of her eye. She could see Lonny get up from the loveseat and walk hesitantly to the open kitchen door, where he knocked twice on the outer wall.

"You want me to change that light for you? I noticed one of the bulbs is out. I can change it if you'd like."

"Well, sure," Rhea told him. She had bought a new bulb months ago, and its white cardboard box stared at her every time she opened the closet door.

Lonny pulled one of the two wooden chairs over to the center of the kitchen and stepped up onto the seat. He began to remove the fixture.

The small wave of relief she felt at having this attended to took Rhea by surprise. It was immediately followed by a small wave of shame. She was ashamed of needing him, of needing a man to step up on a chair for her. Ashamed to admit that her life had been fuller when she had had Gregory there to step on a chair for her.

Four months after that night in the Honda, he had called from France to tell Rhea he was married; he didn't want her to find out some other way. She hadn't spoken to him since that call, but she knew from friends that he and Jeannine were living in an obscure village in Brittany. That made it all the worse for Rhea, knowing that she couldn't blame it on the lure of a glamorous city—knowing that Gregory was willing to spend cold winters in a small and probably boring place, as long as Jeannine was there. She could barely imagine the Gregory she had known being so confidently in love. According to friends, he always said that he and Jeannine were a "yin-yang" couple.

The day he called to let her know he was married, Rhea had gone and canceled all of her weekend plans. She wanted to force herself to be completely alone for a few days, to prove that she didn't need Gregory or anyone else. And she had done it, spent two days and three evenings completely alone. At times it was fine, and at other times she thought she could no longer take it, her head full of the thought that no one loved her anymore, not really, not truly, not the way that Gregory had.

"This light cover's pretty dirty," Lonny said when he had screwed in the new bulb. "Let me wash it for you."

"You don't have to do that."

"I want to." Lonny stepped down from the wooden chair, went to the sink, and rinsed out the globe full of dust and dried-out bugs.

Where was the shame in needing someone? Rhea wondered as she watched him. And yet she continued to feel it.

"Wire's dead," Mike announced, as if it were a groundbreaking discovery. He was a tall, thick-limbed man in a Celtics sweatshirt. He stood next to Lonny in the kitchen and told Rhea, "We're going to have to connect the existing line to the dead outlet. Lonny here will take care of that for you." His bright blue eyes sparkled. Did his sister—Lonny's fiancée—have those eyes, too? Rhea wondered. Mike slammed shut his tool case and left.

"Whew," Lonny said when Mike had gone. "I knew I was right. Well, we'd better work quick. The sun's going down." Even with the new bulb, the kitchen was wan now that the sunlight had gone. Rhea worked in the dusk, while Lonny did his own work across the hall. She could just barely hear him. It was pleasant, the din of human labor. Now she remembered what it had felt like: the comfort of silent, easy company, having someone nearby, with her in a way that was other than social, the two of them toiling away with care and concern. A sensation came to her, familiar in a long-ago way, a reminder of the time when Gregory would revise his papers quietly at his desk while Rhea worked on her dissertation at her own. It was the sensation of shared emotion—in this case a certain relief at having solved a problem, and a sense that something good might come of a bit of work.

When the telephone rang, it sounded louder than usual—an interruption of their quiet, common toil. Rhea made no move to get up, felt no urge to rise from her chair. She heard herself call out, "Would you do me a favor and answer that?"

Lonny appeared at the kitchen doorway, as Rhea added, "Could you tell whoever it is that I've moved?"

Where had the thought come from? Rhea wondered, watching Lonny raise the receiver. She wanted to move, that was it, she wanted to have already moved on, to a place with sockets that didn't burn out, to a place where hard work felt good and paid off, to a place where if you were alone it felt fine, and if you weren't it was even better.

"Umm . . . she moved," Rhea heard Lonny say. "Well, yes, I'm sure. Ummm . . . well, today. Yes, she moved. Uh, no, I don't have the new address. No, I don't have the number." There was a brief silence. "I'm sorry." Lonny hung up. He eyed Rhea doubtfully and said, "That was your landlord."

Rhea began to laugh, first just from her chest and then from her belly. Lonny laughed, too. Then he looked at her in a puzzled way and asked, "Why did you do that?"

"I was feeling really fine right before that phone rang, and I guess I worried it would bring me back to my life." She pursed her lips and added, "I didn't mean for that to sound depressing."

"I'd rather hear that than learn you're on the run from the law." Lonny smiled. "Well, I'd better get back to work."

About thirty minutes later, he was back at the kitchen door.

"All set," he told her. "If you're worried about both sockets being on the same line, you can get a surge protector, but that extension cord should do just fine."

Rhea thanked him and asked how much she owed. Lonny ripped a pink slip off of his clipboard and lowered his head, shaking it slightly. He explained the costs for labor and repairs. "I'm sorry, all that and I couldn't even fix it, really."

"It's my landlord's money, if that makes you feel any better." Rhea handed him a check. He took it and looked at her signature in a lingering way, then put the check in a folder with the repair slip.

"Do you get to go home now?" Rhea asked him.

"Yup. Too late for any more repairs."

Rhea thought about this for a moment and then added, "Will your fiancée be home?"

"Yup." Lonny let his shoulders drop. "I noticed that the top of the window blind was stuck. In the living room. I'll straighten it out for you."

He left the kitchen for a few minutes. Rhea sat back down in front of her computer, but she couldn't refocus on her work. He had been here long enough, she told herself. As soon as he left, she could move back to her desk in the living room, where the westward windows offered each day's last light and stunning sunsets.

Lonny returned, clearing his throat. "Blind's fixed. Every-thing should be fine now."

"Thanks again," Rhea said, and stood up to accompany him to the door.

Lonny walked there slowly. When they passed the fuse box in the entranceway, he looked at the smudged fingerprints left over from Mike's fiddling and said, "Let me wipe this off for you."

"No, no, please don't worry about it." The afternoon had been fine, Rhea thought, but now it was time for him to go. And as if he sensed this, Lonny stepped out of the door, said good night, and was gone.

Rhea closed the door and locked it. She turned back to witness the last moments of sunset through the bay windows of the living room. The sun had already dropped away, but the elongated clouds made red streaks in the sky. Though she had seen such spectacles before, Rhea stood and watched with amazement. She watched for seconds, then minutes, until she realized that the room had become dark. She went to the repaired socket to turn on the torchiere lamp, the one that had indicated the whole elec-trical problem in the first place. Pressing the switch, she braced herself for disappointment, but the lamp sent up its bright rays, and it seemed miraculous: the room lit up with halogen sun.

Anyone out on Commonwealth Avenue could easily see in, Rhea realized, see the large woodblock prints on the walls, see Rhea standing with her hand still on the little switch of the white lamp. Lonny could see her, if he were waiting for the T; it stopped right in front of her building. Rhea walked over to the windows to begin shutting the Venetian blinds. She looked out, but the T must have just left. There was no one there.

Tears welled in Rhea's eyes. And yet it did not seem a bad thing that for a few hours that day—as Rhea now saw quite clearly—the man from Allston Electric had cared about her more than anyone else in the world.

Anniversary

It was ten years ago today that Eileen found herself leaning up against a building on Bowdoin Street, out of breath and barely able to stand. Though she had been smoking happily and basically nonstop for thirty-five years, the inability to breathe came as a shock.

At the hospital, she was asked to blow into a balloon, to make a little arrow rise on a dial. When the dial refused to move, the nurse called in a small charge of doctors, and Eileen could see in their faces that they thought she was about to die. She was too weak to explain that she had decided not to. And so they scurried around in emergency fashion, preparing her deathbed, making the call to her son, wearing serious faces, and treating her with that fearful kindness people affect toward the dying.

And yet here she is, skinny as ever, her bony fingers swollen at the joints, ankles so thin she once broke one just by stepping the wrong way. She is alive. It pleases her to think that she is a statistical improbability, a living refutation of scientific fact. Each morning, rain or shine, winter or spring, she pushes her long feet into orthopedic sneakers and rides her three-speed bicycle down back streets to the foundation in North Cambridge where she works. In the bike's padded basket are the water bottle and thermal container of broth that she takes wherever she goes. She hasn't smoked a cigarette since that day at the hospital.

"You *have* to live," her best friend, Annie, told her back then, "or else Mack will be an orphan." It wasn't a particularly helpful thing to say, and Eileen suspects that Annie, who never had children of her own, would have been more than happy to take over all parenting duties. But Eileen does feel a bit of guilt for putting Mack through such a scare. He was only a sophomore in college the day when they called him from the hospital, and pretty much everything else in his life had been easy. Even now he has that same relaxed, sheltered way about him, though he's almost thirty and should have seen some sort of trouble by now. A week ago he proposed to the wrong woman, who told him yes. Eileen hasn't informed him of his mistake; it's his life, and she refuses to be made to feel responsible for it.

"What happened to that other girl?" Annie asked when she heard the news.

"Oh, she was too much for him." That's Eileen's assessment, although she wishes he had dared to try to make it work. There was something just slightly off-kilter about Rhea, and Eileen liked the way that her occasional bracing comments revealed an unyielding, if submerged, fervor. But she was doomed to the sludgy life of a scholar, misunderstanding and defeat part of her daily grind. It was clear to Eileen that Rhea would always take the more difficult path—which is nothing Mack has ever had the patience for.

Callie, meanwhile, works at a television station. She's the type of dedicated worker—resourceful if not imaginative, smart if not intellectual, quick if not precise—who, Eileen is certain, can succeed at almost anything.

"You know Mack. He's not the type to step up to a challenge. He likes things easy."

He is the product of a great love affair, though you wouldn't know it by looking at him. There's something innocent and carefree about his very movements—sloppy like a puppy. Eileen sees the little boy in him even when he goes through periods of not shaving, even when she walked in on him and Callie that night when they were visiting last summer. He has Eileen's long limbs and his father's messy dark hair, and his usual expression is one of sleepy contentment. To Eileen he looks as if he needs to be nudged.

His father had a puppy-dog quality, too, but more exuberant and purposeful, as if aware every minute that he had only this one shot at life. Eileen met him at a kibbutz a generation ago, back when she was thirty-three and Israel really did need more trees. It was Annie's idea to go there; she had decided to leave her husband and declared that if she didn't go far away she was going to go crazy.

"I knew something was up," Annie says now. They are at the Vietnamese restaurant where they have been dining weekly ever since Annie moved here twelve years ago. The menu has never changed, and the same faded sign hangs on the door: "Please Do Not Double Parking."

"The other day at the gym," Annie tells Eileen, "I was riding the stationary bike, and I looked out the window onto the soccer field, and there was a bride in a gown with a veil and a long white train. Just gliding right across the field, with her dress and the veil billowing behind her."

"Sounds like a ghost." Eileen coils noodles between her chopsticks. Her fingers are long, her nails blunt, the skin at her knuckles cracking slightly.

"No, it was one of the students, a girl in some team uniform, lugging the goal to another part of the field. The net was flowing out behind her, all white and billowy. But for a split second she morphed into a bride."

Eileen nods at Annie's insight. "Callie's one of those athletic types." Tall and rosy, with long legs, swimmer's shoulders, healthful skin, and her hair full of highlights, Callie could be on the cover of a fitness magazine. She and Mack have broken up numerous times but always end up going back to each other.

"It's true I'm a bit psychic," Annie admits, sipping her tea. "Just not in any particularly useful way."

She smooths the enormous, frilly collar of her blouse. Everything Annie wears looks like it has just come out of some attic trunk. She finds things at flea markets and thinks them bargains. Her blouse tonight has frills all the way down the front and billowing sleeves that are too short. Being a professor of philosophy, she can get away with this kind of thing.

She teaches at a college just outside of Boston, which is why Eileen, who used to see her only on visits to New York, first proposed these weekly meetings. Their little table by the window has been the setting for some of their most heated debates. Eileen knows what the owners, a middle-aged couple from Hanoi, think: that she and Annie are aging lesbians, too in love to ever part despite their strong, sometimes loud, differences. One time Eileen brought a co-worker to dine here, and the owner's wife kept giving disturbed looks, as if Eileen were doing something adulterous.

"So—what's she like, really?" Annie asks. "I mean, now that you know she's going to be your daughter-in-law?"

Eileen thinks only a moment before saying, "Her crotch is always showing."

Annie lets out a cackle. "What, is she liberated?"

"She always wears short skirts, and I swear every time I look there's this *view*." Eileen shakes her head at herself, because even though it's true it's not at all what she means.

She tries again: "Last summer, when she and Mack were staying with me, we were going out to dinner and she'd put this tight little peach-colored dress on." But how can she explain? Though she pictures Callie with her hair clipped back in a simple blond ponytail, glowing in her fitted peach dress, there is no way to put into words the way this girl moves, so unaware of her own body, of her physical power. They had reached the bottom of the stairwell when Callie said, "Wait, I need to fix my sandal." But the dress was too tight for her to bend over; without hesitation, Callie hiked it up to her hips. Eileen still sees that peach tutu at her waist, while Callie fiddled with the strap on her sandal. Mack had already opened the door and stepped out onto the street. Anyone could have walked down the stairs right then, anyone on the street could have looked in, but what impressed Eileen was how un-self-consciously Callie had carried herself—and how Mack, waiting on the sidewalk, didn't even notice.

Another time, Callie came to breakfast in nothing but one of Mack's T-shirts and her thong underwear. She went around like that all morning, reading the sports section, making herself more toast when she felt like it.

But none of this explains what Eileen means. She says, "There's this amazing lack of propriety about her." Yes, that's it. "We thought we were like that, Annie, didn't we? Back in our twenties, in our thirties? We wanted to be. We thought we'd told the world to go screw itself, but we were always so *aware* of what we were doing. We were too conscious of ourselves, always making statements. With our lives!" She takes a gulp of tea and thinks of women she used to know, whose divorces were collective acts as much as personal decisions, whose clothes and affairs and careers and sexually transmitted diseases were badges of independence.

She asks, "Are other girls like that now?"

"It's true the girls I teach wear skimpy clothes," Annie says. "I would hate to be a teen nowadays. They think they have to look like something out of a music video."

But that's not Eileen's point, either. She says, "With Callie, it's different, It's nothing she's trying to be, it's just the way she is. It's an amazing thing, actually. I find it inspiring."

"Then what's the problem?"

Eileen digs into her noodles. "With the two of them together, it's just too . . ." She searches for the right word. "Comfortable. You know how Mack is. He needs someone to push his buttons, to get him *going* somewhere. There's no edge to his life. There's nothing to fight for. It's all soft corners and cushy sofas,"

Anniversary

Annie has formed a wicked smile. "I'm sure between the two of us we could find plenty of ways to push his buttons. He doesn't necessarily need a wife to do that." She gives a little snort. "I love to push buttons. I push them all time."

Eileen can't help wondering what Annie's students think of her, with her darting eyes and big, active nostrils, with her cackling laugh and her habit of sometimes talking to herself. "Careful, Annie," she tells her. "You know how you sound when you talk like that. If you don't watch out you're going to end up like the old bat I saw in the drugstore today. She was returning a bottle of hand lotion that she must have had hanging around for at least ten years. The poor guy at the counter didn't know what to do; they don't even make that brand any more."

"I love it," Annie says. "The nerve those old broads have."

With her face thinning out, her chin has somehow gotten longer, and Eileen thinks that in a certain light, from just the right angle, Annie is starting to look like a witch. This is a new, fascinating, development. When she turned sixty-three Annie vowed to no longer dye her hair, and so it is suddenly coarse, frizzy. Her nose is long and curved, and her pouting lower lip, which everyone used to say looked sexy, now just drags her jowls down. Her breasts, too, sag, amazingly so, into her belly when she hunches her shoulders. And yet Annie is still, at the same time, moment to moment, that fiery-cheeked college student who vowed never to wear anything as confining as a bra.

With awe Eileen observes her friend's mutations. She wonders at the way a person goes from being a buxom Bryn Mawr girl singing a cappella to *this*.

Back in their twenties and thirties, Annie was always the attractive one, the big-breasted one, the one people set up on

Calamity

104

dates. No one ever set Eileen up. At the kibbutz Annie had a number of boyfriends and seemed to forget about her husband in no time. Eileen didn't particularly like the other kibbutzniks, mostly Europeans and Scandinavians, all in their twenties, smoking too much dope and spending too much time checking each other out. The men didn't even try to find a solution to the constant power outages, were unwilling even to do something about the stray cats that walked over everything, including the food and dishes and kitchen supplies. The women went around in short-shorts, halter tops, and Dr. Scholl's and worked inefficiently.

"We need more Dafnas," Eileen used to joke, referring to the Israeli women living there. They at least got work done. Eileen could not bear to watch chores take so much longer than they should, could not even stand to watch the many idle flirtations that went nowhere. "Come on, Dafna," she'd tease some Danish girl with her wooden sandals kicked off, drying her hair in the sun, and direct her toward a specific task. Someone had to take charge.

"What this place really needs is passion," she said one day as a young man fiddled with a circuit breaker in the main building. He turned his thick-lashed eyes toward her and seemed to think her brilliant.

"You look like a ballerina." It was the first time he had spoken to her, though she had seen him often enough before, usually helping himself to seconds at the canteen.

"I said 'passion,' not 'euphemism.' " Eileen lit a cigarette and looked at the boy's round face, blue eyes, faint freckles, and messy hair. He was stocky in a robust, bow-legged way.

"To me you're a ballerina," he said, and then walked over to shake her hand. He was from the Midwest and had been taught to do things right.

Eileen wondered just how earnest a person could be. She drew a breath from her cigarette and said, "You must be dehydrated."

The boy laughed. "You can't stand this place, can you?"

"Other kibbutzim can't possibly be like this. Can they?"

"I have no idea. I'm only here because of my friend Louis. It was his idea."

"I'm here thanks to a friend, too."

Eileen told him about Annie's impending divorce, and Len told her about living at home in Iowa with his mother. He was twenty-three years old.

In the next few days, Len made sure to be wherever Eileen was, and Eileen felt a private thrill as the girls in their wooden sandals watched him following her around, lighting her cigarettes with his, whispering things in her ear. He made sure she ate enough; Eileen was the sort of person who, when involved in some other activity, could forget to eat. Len held her hand whenever he could. And yet it was a few days before he kissed her, and a few more before he pulled her into his bed. Everything he did was purposeful, in a clumsy, exuberant, way. In bed at night, every single night, before they closed their eyes in search of sleep, the final thing he did was to take her hand in his.

When they returned to the States, his mother would call Eileen a cradle-robber. Part of the problem was that Eileen looked older than she was. Smoking, little sleep, and too much sun had aged her skin, and there would come a time, a few years later, when people sometimes thought Len was a younger brother or cousin, not her lover, certainly not her husband. But

Eileen was used to being denied her sexuality. Her short-short hair, nonexistent breasts, and political activism had long caused people to assume she was a lesbian, an angry one—too skinny and mean to experience love.

Now that she has become—in everyone else's view—old, she is simply seen as asexual, a bony, wrinkled creature with a cigarette-weakened voice and a brief helmet of gray hair, without physical passions. To Len, back when she was in her thirties, Eileen's skinniness was youthful, her cropped hair radical, her smoker's voice sexy. One day, toward the end of their time in the kibbutz, he said, "I'm going wherever you are."

And so Eileen is forever indebted to Annie for those months of planting trees and eating cucumbers and tomatoes and plain yogurt.

"So—when's the wedding?" Annie is asking.

"Who knows? They haven't decided if they want to do it in San Francisco or back here."

"Too bad old lady Rivlin kicked the bucket," Annie says with a little cackle. "She would have finally gotten to see one of you folks tie the knot." She pauses. "What do you think bothered her more: that you weren't some sweet Midwestern girl, or that you were an unwed mother living in sin?"

Eileen has to smile privately. "I was just so far from anything she had ever imagined for her son."

In his mother's mind, everything had somehow become worse than it was; for years she had Len meeting Eileen at an ashram, a hippie commune, a cult.

"And now," Annie says, "here you are, about to become a mother-in-law." She nods her head so that her eyes look wicked. "Isn't life grand?"

Anniversary

They were together three years before Mack was born. Len worked for a city planning department, while Eileen directed an after-school program in Arlington. Summer weekends they drove to the Catskills to stay in a cabin owned by the parents of Len's friend Steven. There was a lake just small enough to swim across and still be able to make it back, and they spent hours swimming and floating on inflatable rafts that were always leaking. Eileen bought a little watertight plastic case that she clipped to her swimsuit and in which she kept her cigarettes and a lighter. She and Len would lie in privacy on the other side of the lake until they had had enough of a break from Steven's parents, and then Eileen would smoke a cigarette to fortify her lungs for the swim back.

"Time for a toast," she says now. "It's ten years to the day that I scared all those doctors and didn't die." *Decided to keep living* is what she means. But Eileen has no taste for melodrama.

She raises her little mug of tea. Annie raises her beer to say, "And quit smoking. Cold turkey. No small feat."

When Eileen returned from the hospital, Annie did all sorts of things to aid her nonsmoking campaign and keep her busy and distracted: peeled carrot sticks, chopped celery, bought her Tic Tacs and sugar-free chewing gum, told her, "You *have* to live," as if expecting she wouldn't. But Eileen had made up her mind, and though her body's cravings were at first almost unbearable, quitting wasn't at all as difficult as everyone had always made it out to be.

This is true, Eileen has noticed, for most things in life.

Calamity

When she gave birth to Mack, when she was thirty-six, Len was beside her, holding her hand.

A few months later, Len began to get headaches. He had never been the sort to complain, and so neither of them worried until the black spots crept into his vision. He had already had the first surgery when, one night in bed, he took her hand and Eileen realized that his grasp felt different. Weak, that was it, as if something had been drained out of him. Eileen let go of his hand and sat up.

"What's wrong?" Len asked, and it was the one and only instant in which Eileen did not tell him the truth—that she was, for the first time in her life, terrified.

A CAT scan revealed an image Eileen will never escape from: Len's body riddled with tumors. They were everywhere, undeniable. Within a day he could barely lift his arms. Then it was his bowed legs that lay heavy and useless. Eileen made phone calls, brought Annie in from New York, asked friends to take charge of the baby, listened as Len's voice faltered along with his thoughts. She sat beside him feeling as if she were in a play or a movie, trying to concentrate on her role, not fully understanding that this was real, yet perfectly aware of what she was not yet understanding. Len didn't seem to understand, either. At times he spoke clearly, but never about what was happening. He mentioned repairs he meant to make in the apartment, a check he had forgotten to mail, a joke Steven had told him. Eileen held his hand, felt its strength fluctuate and diminish. Her mind kept trying to adjust, readjusting, while Len daily became someone new

His mother had arrived. She sat on the other side of the hospital bed shaking her head, her mouth a tight twist of disapproval, as if Eileen were personally responsible for this disaster.

By then Len was talking nonsense. Two days later, he was dead. And so, for a while, the apartment was frequented by their friends, crying and asking questions and hugging Eileen while she, too, cried, and holding little Mack so Eileen could take breaks to shower and sob. Annie ran around sighing and cooking heavy meals.

"Thank God for Mack," Eileen kept saying in those first few months, as she waded through days that seemed to be measured in something longer than time. The world itself was suddenly opaque, as if set apart from Eileen by a thick film, something she could almost touch. Only Mack, with his cheerful, clueless face and joyful eyes, pulled her like a towrope through slow, unending hours.

Even now Eileen is often amazed by what it means, for so many people, to keep living: to awake each morning startled by alarm clocks, to stir spirals into coffee and shove feet into shoes. She has puzzled over the fact of so much accumulated time spent licking stamps, moving trash from one place to another, storing summer clothes and unfolding winter ones. Kitchen sponges, magazine subscriptions, doctors' appointments, birthday cards, nail clippers, checkbooks. When she chose to live, that day at the hospital ten years ago, she knew that her decision meant, as much as anything else, all of these things.

When everyone had left and she was alone with Mack and without Len—that was when Eileen felt a new kind of sadness. Sometimes it was an enormous hole in her stomach and sometimes it was a sharp twisting in her heart. Sometimes it was a sudden pulse that shot through her limbs and almost caused her to cry out. Always it was a heavy ache in her chest. Throughout the day she carried with her this ache. Eileen was thankful for it. She was thankful for what it meant: She was living. Not since falling in love, not since giving birth, had she felt so fully, physically, aware of being alive.

The owner's wife has returned with their change, delivered to them on a little plastic tray. It also holds two mints wrapped in plastic. Eileen and Annie trade money back and forth, rise, tuck in their chairs, wish their hosts good night.

Outside, the sun is setting. Now that the clocks have been turned forward, the evenings are longer and the avenue has filled with people, mostly young, making the most of the season.

"You have a good weekend, Eileen."

"You too kiddo."

Eileen finds her bicycle and is still working the combination on her lock when Annie calls, "Just give me a ring if you need some buttons pushed!"

Eileen waves as Annie turns and continues toward her car. From behind, without the frills of her blouse, without her changing face, Annie could be anyone, at any point in time.

The spring air tastes sweet, and the little peppermint is almost spicy on Eileen's tongue. Eileen pulls on her reflective vest and rolls up a pant cuff. She weaves in and out of traffic on her bicycle. Only in the past year has she begun wearing a helmet. It was a gift from Mack—a number of years ago, actually, but at first Eileen refused to wear it, like those hockey players back in the eighties who, while their teammates were forced to don the new standard-issue headgear, skated around vainly with their hair flapping, exempt from rules, older and tougher than everyone else.

A misty rain has started, the delicate, light-scented kind that only happens in springtime. It feels good on Eileen's face. The moisture darkens the streets and sidewalk, and as the last of the sun slips away, the streetlights glow. With gratification, Eileen chews the last of her peppermint. The rain is coming down faster now. Sidewalks glisten.

It was raining the night they spent in Blois, the first stop on their trip to the Loire Valley. This was the one vacation she and Len took together, in August, three years after they met. The little restaurant where they ate was low-ceilinged and lit by nothing but candles. With the door of the restaurant's entrance open, Eileen could see right onto the street, where puddles splattered and couples stopped for shelter in little cavelike doorways of stone. She and Len sat drinking red wine, their knees touching under the little table, warm and dry, their pleasure magnified by the fact of the wet, cold world just outside the door, so close they could smell it.

At her building, Eileen locks her bicycle and reflective vest behind the stairwell. She climbs the stairs to her apartment, unclicks two locks, flicks on a light, tosses the day's mail onto a chair. In the bathroom she washes her face, then brushes her teeth briefly, though they never look quite clean and her gums always cause the dentist to make all sorts of worrisome comments.

That day in Blois, they had admired the cathedral and the old sundial and eaten avocado sandwiches at a park overlooking the

Loire. But when they stepped out of the little restaurant into the rain that night, the scent that greeted them was of autumn: wet leaves, chilled clouds, gray air. On the way back to the hotel, they got lost and rain poured over them. Len said, "This town looks better wet."

Eileen enters her bedroom, unbuttoning her damp shirt. Before pulling the window curtains shut, she looks out at the street. There is always someone there, no matter how late, no matter how foul the weather. Sometimes there are lovers walking hand in hand, sometimes a group of drunkards singing. Tonight Eileen sees a lone person trudging through puddles, laden with heavy bags.

She watches until the figure has passed, then unlaces her leather sneakers, pulls off her socks, her pants, her shirt. She tosses her underwear at the laundry bin and slips into the cotton nightgown that has been washed so many times it feels like the finest silk. She turns down the covers of her bed.

Even now Eileen sometimes dreams about Len. Most often these are regular, uneventful scenes in which he is flipping an omelet or singing a silly song. When she wakes up she thinks, for a few blurry seconds, that she is young and that Len is beside her. And then the hollow stab fills her stomach. But it is much duller and briefer than it was decades ago.

In the hotel, Eileen shocked the owner with a request for hot chocolate. He was closing the restaurant for the night and said so, frowning. But then, a few minutes later, he arrived at their room with two steaming cups on a wooden tray.

Eileen takes a sip of water from a plastic cup and climbs into bed, pleasingly tired from the long day and her ride home with the rain in her face. She still wonders what caused the man's change of heart, wonders if he somehow divined the truth. They were on honeymoon. But they hadn't told anyone.

Their room was a tiny L with pale, striped wallpaper and a dorm room's simplicity: wooden desk, metal lamp, nondescript chair. The little strip of full-length mirror tacked to the door made Eileen look even skinnier than she was. The bed was small and firm, the down pillows round and extremely soft. From under his thick eyelashes, Len gave her his roguish look. It was one of the private things they had between them, one of the few things no one else knew.

The breeze stirs the window curtains and touches her lightly. Lying on her back, she lets her head weigh into the thin pillow and clasps her hands together, one over the other. Anyone looking in, seeing her lying there, might think her a corpse posed for a coffin. But against her palms Eileen feels her pulse slowly pumping. She feels the warmth of one hand in another.

Snapshots

This was Jean's first summer in Oregon and she swore it would be her last. The air was too breezy, too mild. She liked weather to match her moods: overbearing heat, languid humidity, wild summer storms like they had back east. I had spent the summer trying to please her, and now that the temperature had made it to the eighties, I'd suggested we eat lunch out back. I was carrying a tray of sandwiches across our lawn—a hill of dry weeds, brown and stubbled as a hedgehog's back. The grass crunched under my feet. Eli always cut it too short.

Jean was already comfortable on a cotton blanket, propped up on one arm, eating a nectarine. It was a perfect picture, her tan shoulders above the pale pink blanket, the sunrays stroking her sleek brown hair. I couldn't see her eyes through her black sunglasses. I thought she was looking at me, and I smiled. But she was looking at our back porch. She said, "Jesus, Geoff. What an ugly house."

She could talk that way because she didn't own it. Eli did, and took painstakingly destructive care of it. In fact, he was in it that very moment, tampering with our toilet. He liked to stop by and let himself in. That day we had revealed to him, reluctantly, that the toilet was leaking. He was our landlord, after all. But Eli had a way of standing in front of broken appliances and scratching his head.

Jean had said under her breath, "Some people call the *plumber.*" But that wasn't Eli's style. He fancied himself a handyman even if no one else did. He would make surprise visits to install window shades or light fixtures, and after he left we would have to replace sockets with the proper bulbs, or take down the blinds and turn them around the way they were meant to be.

Jean would never forgive me for having rented a place full of jammed windows and faulty wiring. I didn't let on what I had come to suspect—that Eli had constructed the entire house himself. On a shelf in the basement I'd found a well-ruffled manual, *The Weekend Carpenter Builds His Own Home.* I accepted the possibility that our living quarters were entirely the product of Eli's handiwork. There were the too-steep stairs, the odd-shaped kitchen, the awkward little balcony that protruded from the face of the house like a large mole. We were surrounded by blunders. Cabinets and drawers opened into one another, and locks turned backward, but how was a prospective tenant to notice such quirks? I was too excited at the idea that Jean and I were actually moving in together; I'd never lived with a girlfriend before. I'd relocated to Oregon for a job I'd started in March, back when

Jean was still finishing grad school, and so the house hadn't had to pass muster with her. I was awed by the view of Mount Hood, by the sloping backyard, by the big rooms and low rent. Eli seemed dependable, and the view of the city, over the green hills of the Northwest, was spectacular.

Of course, being in the hills meant we had poor radio and TV reception. More precisely, we received the Christian station and nothing else. Jean was patient about this. She was comforted by the fact that we had never signed a lease or given any sort of deposit. Eli, and all of Oregon, it seemed, worked on an honor system.

On the first floor of the house, in a smaller apartment, lived a man named Stefan. Neither his nationality nor his line of work was clear, and this made Jean nervous. Sometimes she put her ear to the floorboards to try to listen in on his conversations. All she managed to pick up were the smells of what he cooked—ground beef, garlic, burnt toast. It seemed normal enough to me, but Jean was suspicious; large, muscular men occasionally came by to drive Stefan places. I hadn't noticed them until Jean moved in.

She was twenty-five. We'd spent the past year long-distance, with me still in California and Jean in New York, where she had been invited to join a prestigious art program. Now was the first time in her life that she was no longer a student, and though she had complained about the university until the moment they handed her an M.F.A., she was suddenly sure that she didn't belong anywhere else. She had no job. She was an artist, a painter, and though she had been a young star back east, nobody knew her out here. She convinced herself her work was no good, said she had to start from scratch. She spent hours each day on a project that she insisted would be better than anything she had ever done. That big piece of taut canvas was the one thing she cared about. She sat on the warped floor of the screened-in back porch mixing thick oil paints into glistening peaks, and then she would burst out with how bad it all was, how she couldn't create in this weather, how there wasn't enough sun, how the floor sloped.

But that Sunday she looked happy, lying on the pale pink blanket. This was the way it was meant to be, I thought, and for the first time all summer I felt that something good was in our grasp. Jean said, "What an ugly house," and I wanted to show camaraderie. I looked at the lopsided porch, its thickly layered paint and splintered steps, and agreed. Jean said, as an afterthought, "Eli needs to raise the blade on the lawn mower."

We ate the sandwiches and fed the crumbs to the dead grass. Jean laid her head in my lap. I massaged her scalp. I was still under the impression that I could somehow make her happy.

Later I sneaked into the garage and changed the blade on the lawn mower.

I came home from work to find Jean listening to the radio; she liked to laugh at the talk shows. I gave her a kiss while, in quick confident motions, she shucked ears of white corn. "You've got to listen to this shit," she said.

A husband had called in to discuss how his wife had begun to read crime novels for hours every night, and how he suspected she was trying to avoid him. The radio announcer suggested he look to God for help and provided a sample prayer.

I said, "It's also kind of sad."

Jean kissed the back of my neck and pinched my rear. She was good at moves like that—fast, loving ones that came out of nowhere and that twenty seconds later you'd swear you must have imagined.

There was a knock on the kitchen door. Stefan was standing on the back porch among Jean's canvases and supplies, eyeing her work skeptically.

The painting was there, the one she had so much hope for. It was a large canvas on which she made gradual additions of color so subtle that I at times couldn't even tell what changes had been made. I felt useless that way. In the three years that we had been together, my competency as an appreciator of art had never seemed to matter, but now here was Jean, away from her New York art school friends and from the people she had known in California; I felt it my duty to encourage her.

Stefan nodded at the broad canvas politely when he saw me. Jean was putting a pot of water on to boil. I opened the flimsy wooden door and greeted Stefan. He always looked dapper, in a European way—his jeans ironed, his shoes leather and polished. I don't think it had occurred to me that he was handsome. He said, in an unplaceable accent, "I was wondering if I could borrow your wife."

"Excuse me?" I glanced at Jean, though we weren't even married. She was still listening to the radio, laughing at someone's problems.

"A knife," Stefan said, patiently. "May I borrow one of your knives?"

Jean said, "Hi there, Stefan. Come on in."

I told her, "Stefan just needs to borrow a knife."

"Well, sure, though I don't know how good any of them are. I mean, who knows when any of them were last sharpened."

"What kind of a knife would you like?" I asked Stefan, hoping to intone that we had no qualms when it came to lending sharp implements to dubious neighbors.

"A big one would be preferable."

"A big one," repeated Jean. "Well, I'd say this is the biggest we've got." She pulled a wide silver knife from the slanted wood block.

"That's perfect," said Stefan. "I appreciate it."

Jean handed him the knife, and it's that image that sticks in my mind, the way she passed it to him, blade down, with wavering prudence. It was as though, careful as she was with it, at any minute she might betray herself and do some sort of damage. She had a sudden frightened look, as if she too had just recognized that possibility in herself. I can still see Jean's muscular arm outstretched. For a split second I truly believed the knife would never make it into Stefan's grip. But Jean looked Stefan in the eye and handed it over. Stefan thanked us and said, "I'll bring it right back."

I was in a good mood, because I'd figured out Stefan's profession. We'd just passed each other near the firm where I worked. When I asked what he was doing downtown, Stefan said, "I work here," and pointed to the building behind him. "I'm a detective."

The building was one of the older ones, with a respectable brick façade and a touch of grime. There was no signage to indicate its use, but Stefan was proud to talk about it. It was a bond company he worked for. He was a bounty hunter. He described how he tracked down people who had skipped bail and, opening the door of a car parked at the curb, took out a pair of handcuffs and a white bulletproof vest. I worried he might blow his cover, but I guess he didn't have one.

That's what I was thinking about on my way to meet Jean. She had found a job as a part-time graphic designer. It paid peanuts, and she alternately liked and hated it. Some nights we would meet at a small bar we liked, where the drinks were a little too strong.

When I walked in, I couldn't find her. I sat on a less-than-clean bar stool and chatted with the bartender. He was new, and he talked the sort of never-ending babble that bartenders usually just listen to. A petite blonde woman came and sat on the stool next to me.

I was looking for a way out of the bartender's soliloquy. He was going on about the various women who had done him wrong, and the blonde was nodding along, as if she knew exactly what he meant. "So you know how it is, do you?" I asked her. That was how it started, the blonde woman checking me out, me checking her out. It felt good to flirt. For a moment I feared Jean would see us—me leaning into the concave of the blonde woman's body, the tips of her long hair grazing my arm. And then I realized that I wanted her to see.

She walked in briskly, so that I saw her easily from the corner of my eye. I touched the woman's back, I don't know why. Briefly, but long enough. Jean saw.

She didn't stop short, catch herself mid-step, look shocked, or stare at the blonde woman. None of that. Jean just raised her eyebrows. Her eyelids slid down a bit over her dark eyes in that amused way they had. I doubt she'd remember, but it was the look she had given me when I asked her, in the crowded coffee shop the day we met, if I might join her at her table. That's the picture I see in my mental scrapbook. That same skeptical look.

And I was proud when Jean walked up to us confidently and gave me an equally confident kiss. The blonde woman made herself invisible in a showy way and left the bar soon after. Jean refused to mention her, and instead we talked about good news: Jean's work was being considered for an exhibit.

"In Miriam Choi's gallery. She saw some of my stuff in New York last year, and she's interested. She's going to come over and have a look. I told her I was almost done with *Happy Family*."

"What's that?"

"My painting. The one you bump into every time you walk through the porch. It's called *Happy Family*. I have to finish it. She's going to try to review my stuff next month sometime. I'm so lucky she happened to go to my show last year."

It was good to see Jean enthusiastic. The painting could bring that out in her, and I was sure that if it would just turn out the way she hoped, if she could just be pleased with the outcome, she would feel good about herself and we would be happy.

We sat at the bar relishing our mutual contentment. For about two hours we were having a good time, and for the next two hours we were still having a good time but in a fearful way, knowing it would have to end. We were determined not to let it. We kept eating bar food and drinking.

When it was time for the place to close, Jean said she didn't want to go home. "Sometimes that house just gives me the creeps. For all I know, Eli's there drilling holes or something." Then she said, "Sometimes I just can't bear walking into that house." So I told her, "Fine, let's not go home."

We went to one of the parks, I don't remember which one; there were a lot like that, with a basketball court, a baseball field, benches, homeless people, and restrooms that smelled. We made out on a bench. It must have been 3 a.m.

We slept there, under a tree in the park. It was chilly, and the grass was damp, and the tree roots were like knuckles in my side. Tucked into each other's arms, we yawned at the night dew and shivered ourselves to sleep. In my dreams I saw Jean looking at me the way she had in the bar, the way she had on the day we met. When we woke up it was six, and people had already begun jogging and walking dogs. Jean didn't complain when I suggested we go home.

I was chopping a large onion and having trouble; Stefan still had our big knife, and neither Jean nor I felt like asking him about it. A Styrofoam coffee cup, an empty doughnut box, and a sports magazine lay on the kitchen table. They weren't ours. Somebody had been in our house. At first we'd assumed it was Eli, though there were no signs of immediate damage. We turned on faucets with caution, looked warily for nails underfoot. We'd briefly wondered if it had to do with Stefan, but he didn't seem the doughnut-eating sort.

Though I'd told her all I knew about him, Jean still thought

Stefan suspicious. She insisted she had heard odd noises coming from below—a sound like a dull saw going back and forth. She talked about it enough that I myself had begun to wonder: perhaps Stefan posed some sort of threat.

But for the moment we let Stefan off the hook, abandoned the investigation. We had other things on our minds. Jean had just finished throwing a tantrum—brief and fierce as a tropical storm. No specific reason, just the general state of our life together. Just my humming or putting a dish in the wrong cabinet could set her off. We were growing tired of each other, though at the time we wouldn't have even considered that a possibility.

Now Jean was listening to the Christian station, nodding along as she macerated a clove of garlic. I watched her pick up the phone and dial a number.

"I wish our fights didn't always end with you ignoring me," I said, sweeping the onion into a frying pan. "I wish we could kiss and make up."

"Hi, I'm calling in response to what Hal from Corvallis said? I think—Jean. Yes, I'll hold."

I said, "I'm standing right here, Jean. If you want to talk about it, let's talk about it."

"Quiet. They're putting me on the air."

"Jean—"

"Hi. Jean. Portland. Hi, I just wanted to say that I agree with Hal, and I have some advice for him. . . . My background? Well, let's see. I, too, am married—How long? Forever. Ha ha. No, actually I've been married, let's see . . . eleven years. Eleven years. To the most wonderful man, and I'd say we've had a very successful marriage, so—Oh, do I? Well, thank you, we got married young. But my husband—His name? Well . . . Eli. Oh, he's a carpenter. Yeah, he built everything in our house . . . even the twins' bunk beds. Yes, it is convenient. He chops the wood himself. In fact, he grows the trees. We have a tree farm. He's something of a Paul Bunyan type. You know, big and muscular, hairy, wears flannel."

I turned to Jean. "I hope I at least get equal airtime." She listened into the receiver for a moment. "Well, what I want to tell Hal is, frankly, I was worried by his blind trust of his wife. Yes. I was concerned about his reluctance to discuss with her the problems he mentioned. Communication is everything, Hal. You need to be as open and honest as possible. Because, take it from me, you have no idea what kind of things your wife might be keeping from you."

I stared at Jean. I allowed myself to wonder—in a brief flicker of thought—about Stefan, and, just as quickly, pushed the idea out of my mind.

Jean listened into the receiver for a moment. "Well, sure, shared faith is important, but that's just a tiny part of it. And I mean, let's face it, no marriage is worth it if you don't have great sex." Jean turned to me, unfazed. "They cut me off."

"Look, Jean, just tell me what you want. If it's the house you hate so much, we'll move. If it's the weather, we'll leave. All right? Will that help?"

She said, "You can't just run away. It's like I told Hal from Corvallis. You can't hide from problems. You have to try to work them out."

But what was there to work out? Jean refused to believe that things happened from within, that a person could cry for no reason, that people fall out of love. In fact, this happens all the time.

People become angry about something that yesterday made them merely shrug. A man looks at a woman he once loved and decides she is incorrigibly ugly.

This was nothing I could accept. If only, I told myself, I could have laughed at her phone call, been in on the joke. But it was her joke, not mine.

They came banging on the door at 2 a.m. I was so tired I didn't even hear it, but Jean, still half asleep, undid the latch. She didn't even ask who it was. The next thing I knew she was shaking me. "Geoff, wake up." Her hair covered her shoulders. I squinted up at her and she asked, "Is Stefan in here?"

"No. Why?"

"The police are wondering."

I got up to talk to them. Jean was already falling back asleep, crawling back under the covers.

The police wouldn't tell me why they wanted Stefan, but they assured me that we were in no personal danger. I assumed it had to do with the bounty hunting. I was too tired to explain it to Jean. At any rate, she was asleep. The next morning she said, "I had a dream about people banging on the door. Men in uniform."

I said, "Oh, really? Tell me about it," but she claimed she couldn't remember. I was sure she knew she hadn't dreamt it. It was just her way of taunting me, seeing how much I dared not to tell her. I played along, saying nothing. She was flaunting secrecy, testing the limits of reticence.

Later, out of the blue, Jean remembered something she'd been meaning to tell me. "I got the knife back from Stefan."

. . .

I'd come home earlier than usual and stopped out front to ad-
mire a particularly large slug. Our car was coming from the other
direction, Jean driving and someone else in it. I straightened up,
my shoes sinking into the soaked grass. The mud smelled ripe.

Jean parked in front of me, and I watched a plump gray-
haired woman emerge from the passenger's side. A baggy silk
outfit covered her in dark folds. She held out her hand and said,
"Miriam Choi."

"Hi, I'm—"

The car door slammed, and Jean said, "This is Geoff," a bit
dismissively, I thought. It occurred to me that perhaps she had
wanted me out of the picture. Now Miriam would associate her
with some guy who hung around on the curb examining slugs.

"How do you do."

"Come on up, Miriam," Jean was saying. "There's a beautiful view of the hills." Upstairs, she unlocked the door to our
apartment. Eli was asleep on the couch.

He sat up when he heard us enter. "Oh," Jean said calmly.
"Miriam, this is Eli."

Eli looked young for his age—or older than his age, depend-
ing on which of his features you focused on. That is, we had no
idea how old he really was. His pudgy, square-jawed face could
seem so tired and strained you'd think he'd look ten years
younger if he just got some rest. But then, if you decided that the
lines on his face were from age rather than from fatigue, you
might think that he was in relatively good shape, still youthful,
his round cheeks still boyish, his hair not entirely gray,

Snapshots

On this particular day he was looking about thirty-five. His painter's pants were muddy, and he had taken off the security-lens glasses he always wore. He ignored Miriam, rubbed his eyes, and asked, "Is Stefan in here?"

"What is it with Stefan?" I demanded. "The police were asking the same thing a few weeks ago."

"Yeah," said Eli. "They told me. They said that they sometimes come in the middle of the night, since there's a better chance the person will be home. Or did you see them the day they had their little stakeout?"

I recalled the doughnut box and the *Sports Illustrated*. Jean became tense. Not only were we ruining her business meeting, but it was possible her personal safety was in peril. "Is he a wanted criminal or something?" she asked. "Because if he is I think we have a right to know. Our lives could be in danger."

"No, no, no," Eli assured us. "I've been looking into it, and it seems he's just not yet a U.S. citizen and his visa is expired or something. Those were immigration guys you saw. He just has to get his papers in order, but I think he's been avoiding it. You know, hiding from the authorities. That's what I want to talk with him about."

Jean shook her head in a way that indicated both sympathy and vexation. "I'm sorry about this, Miriam. Here, let me take your coat."

"I was wondering what he was up to," I said to Eli, taking off my jacket and following Jean to the coat closet. She had opened the door and was looking perturbed.

Stefan was huddled in the closet, the least dapper I had ever seen him.

"This is Stefan," Jean said to Miriam, and handed Stefan

both of the coats. She touched Miriam's elbow. "Why don't we go out to the studio, and I'll show you what I've been working on."

Jean walked away with Miriam, who looked only slightly confused. Stefan poked out his head. "Are the police gone?"

"They're gone. You can come out now." I turned to Eli for corroboration. Eli said, "There are no immigration officials here, Stefan."

Trying not to sound flustered, I said, "I understand that you have keys to the apartment, Eli, but, Stefan, how did you get in here?"

Stefan pushed back the bottom of the longer coats to reveal a large hole in the back of our closet. "I carved a tunnel," he whispered with affected generosity, hoping, I guess, that if Eli heard him he would consider it an improvement and not make him pay for damage.

"Stefan," Eli said, "we need to straighten this thing out." I watched Stefan step out from among my coats and Jean's jackets and wondered at what had happened to my home. It had been transformed into a stakeout for cops, a secret tunnel for fugitives, and, to top it off, the back porch had become a "studio." But what bothered me more was how Jean had introduced me to Miriam. With that same exasperated tone: This is Geoff, Eli, Stefan. As if I were just one of so many troublesome men in her life. She hadn't bothered to explain that I was the important one. That I, not Eli or Stefan, lived there. That I had more claim than either of them to this bit of space. And to her.

.   .   .

For hours on end, Jean would sit next to a space heater on the porch, putting the finishing touches on *Happy Family*. The storm windows were permanently fogged. Her completed works sat draped in white sheets around her. *Happy Family* sat in front of her like a king among the plebeians—bigger and brighter, full of ambitious dreams.

Jean was still waiting to hear from the gallery. I was convinced it would be a yes, since Miriam had made such encouraging comments, but Jean had begun to prepare herself for the worst. Whenever the phone rang she jumped. She wouldn't answer it, because she was afraid of receiving bad news. She listened to the Christian station for hours at a time.

When I came home that day she was in the living room, crying. I assumed it had been a no. "Did Miriam call?" I asked timidly.

"No," she answered. "Who cares about Miriam."

I went over to hold her, asked her what was wrong.

"Everything," she said. Everything was wrong with the house. If she could just get out of it, she said.

She thrust something into my hand. It was a wedding photo, dusty and scratched. Looking closer, I saw that the man was Eli, looking especially boyish, with a shiny-eyed bride at his side. Even with a tux on he wore those thick-lensed security-style glasses. Behind him was the same house we were in now, though in much better shape, still wearing its original coat of paint.

"It was years ago," Jean said. "They lived together in this house."

"I didn't even know Eli was married."

"Divorced. She took the kids and moved to some other state. Stefan said that's what Eli told him."

"Where did you get the photo?"

"I found it in the tunnel. It must have fallen through a crack a long time ago."

"The tunnel?"

"In the closet."

"What were you doing in the tunnel?!"

"Nothing. I was curious."

"Curious? Jean, you could get hurt!"

It was when she grabbed back the photo that I noticed her wrists. The skin was indented, red from friction.

"What are these marks?"

She sighed, bored. "Stefan was showing me his handcuffs."

I stared at her. "What the hell is going on with you and Stefan?"

"I was spying. He caught me."

"You've been spying on Stefan?"

She started crying again. "I thought he might be a threat to us or something. I wanted to know what he was doing."

"Why can't you just sit back and mind your own business? Why are you always looking for something to worry about? Why are you always poking around for something bad?" I took a deep breath. "What did he do to you?"

"He didn't notice until today. Anyway, he's harmless. We were just playing. He taught me some self-defense moves. How can you be thinking of Stefan at a time like this?" She cried harder. "Don't you see?" Jean held out the picture. "A picture can't preserve anything."

Angry and confused as I was, I wanted to show understanding. I looked at the snapshot and said, "You're right. Nothing can bring a photo back to life."

She said, "Everyone knows that." She stood up and walked through the kitchen, through the back door, onto the porch. I didn't realize she had taken the big silver knife from the butcher block.

She slashed the painting in half, then again and again. I found her when it was already too late. When I asked her what she was doing, she just said, "What an ugly picture. I can't stand how ugly it is."

I didn't tell her to stop. I knew how good destruction can feel, like knocking a pile of building blocks to the ground.

"This house is bad luck," Jean said before she moved out. And I wanted to believe it. It was what we both wanted. We needed to blame ourselves on something. All the pain and meanness within us—blame it on something else.

Difficult Thoughts

I met them in Florence, where a halfhearted research proposal had won me six months to translate the work of some fifteenth-century nuns. I'd been through a rough time and would have gone anywhere, really. Though the grant was meager, I felt grateful and worked hard.

I was taking a break at a café not far from the library, reading through my notes and sipping my habitual herb tea. The only caffeine-free kind there was chamomile, and Italians were always assuming I was sick. It didn't occur to me that I in fact looked sick. I'd always been skinny and in the past few months had become even more so; an unexpected trauma before leaving for Italy had left me especially drained. I ate one meal a day, stayed up late squinting into dictionaries, and spent far too much time in an unheated stone library. But when Marcello, smoking at the next table, leaned over and said gleefully, "You're ill?" I blamed the chamomile. I told him and his older brother, Massi, about the dank library, about the poor circulation in my hands, about trying to avoid caffeine. They looked at me with intense interest, the way people do foreigners; in truth it was not my nationality but the notebook, the library, the worrying about caffeine that they found so fascinatingly alien.

We would meet for drinks and outings. Massi and I held hands surreptitiously in the back seat of a Fiat while Marcello drove us on doleful excursions to medieval towns. Marcello's girlfriend had recently left him, and the brothers' impromptu vacation, taken even though classes at their university had resumed, was meant to be therapeutic.

Marcello was overweight and usually suffering from some unnoticeable ailment. The slope of his shoulders gave him a look of perpetual surrender. He sat on the hood of the car pouting into a cigarette while Massi and I climbed hilly trails or crooked stone towers together. One afternoon Marcello looked up from a coffee he was limply stirring and announced that he was scheduled to take an exam at his school—two and a half hours away—that evening. "I really should go," he said, "or this will be the third year in a row I fail the course." The brothers put the top back on the convertible, invited me to come visit them in La Spezia, and drove away.

It would have been easy to never see them again. But even in their absence I would see them, when I should have been concentrating on things like fifteenth-century nuns. I would be thumbing through a musty book of religious verse and Massi would appear, tall and tired, with a gaunt, unimpressed face. His teeth were stained from coffee and tobacco, and his eyes already had little wrinkles around them that made him look pensive. I decided that was what had attracted me—the idea of him having strained his mind over difficult thoughts. Marcello's face was round and soft, with dimpled cheeks that, to me, indicated less serious contemplation.

Too many cigarettes and late nights had aged their skin, though really they were both younger than me. As winter overtook Tuscany, I missed their company. The radiator in my apartment began to rattle violently, and the nuns' poems had taken on a humorous quality that I knew shouldn't have been there. Then I really did get sick. It was just a cold, but chamomile tea could do nothing more for me. I convinced myself that the weather was warmer and brighter everywhere else. I remembered Massi's hand on my right thigh in the back seat of the Fiat. When it had rained for eight days straight and my cold showed no sign of waning, I bought a ticket to visit the brothers.

La Spezia turned out to be a naval port, lined by orange trees that bore inedible fruit, and square gray buildings built by fascists. The structures sulked over their chipped paint and cracked cement. Grizzled cats lurked in doorways and sills. The rain spat sideways. On the side of a main roadway, across from the shuddering ocean, sat Massi and Marcello's apartment, rooted like a grim, oversized Lego piece. The building looked dirty, until I went inside. Its lobby held an elevator as beautiful as anything I'd seen in Florence—velvet carpet, gold-framed mirror, door of gold-plated bars that swirled into vines and nests of flowers. Lifting me to the top floor, its cables heaved with a raspy, incomprehensible whisper.

. . .

"Your timing is perfect," Massi kept saying. We were sitting on a black leather sofa, consciously refraining from showing affection in front of Marcello; he was still (like me, I supposed) in emotional recovery. "This may be my last weekend home. It looks as though I start my military duty on Wednesday."

"It's mandatory, you know," Marcello put in, surprisingly energetic. My fatigue and congestion had brightened his spirits. He was rifling through a cardboard chest, extracting unlabeled pillboxes and little colored vials. "But there are ways out of it," he said. "Technically, all men between the ages of seventeen and twenty-seven must do ten months of military or civil service, so I have two years to figure out how to avoid it."

Massi shook his head like a veteran. "It's not so easy."

"I've been making some phone calls," Marcello said mysteriously, and dissolved an aspirin into his bourbon. He propped my legs up on the couch and handed me a bright red lozenge. "One every two hours. I'm going to prepare a hot-water bottle for your feet." He placed the medicine box on the ebony coffee table, and someone's forgotten wine rippled in its glass.

Massi took advantage of his brother's absence to stroke my shoulder for a minute. I held his other hand and noted its smooth, uncallused palm. It was a rich man's hand. A hand that didn't know work. Even my own hands had faint signs of toil: paper cuts from research, blisters from the strap of my travel bag, chapped skin thanks to my angry radiator. I waited for Massi to say something forthright or candid, or at least about me. Instead he lit a cigarette. Through the balcony window I could see a thick night sky. "It's nice here," I said, for conversation. "Is this where you grew up?"

"We moved to this apartment about ten years ago. My father bought it to please my mother. Then he went off with his girlfriend. They live in Martinique. His company has business there. He sends us a check every month."

It wasn't what I'd had in mind, but it was probably the most revealing thing he had said to me. I heard Marcello returning and let go of Massi's hand, wondering when I would feel it next. Marcello presented me with a hot-water bottle and a blanket, and I lay on the couch like a spoiled invalid. My attendants stood above me smoking cigarettes and telling me how nice it was to see me.

Still on my workingman's schedule, I awoke early the next morning. I followed sounds coming from the kitchen to find a dark-skinned woman shelling tiny green peas. She looked only slightly surprised to find me standing there in a T-shirt and pajama bottoms. "I'm Rhea," I told her.

In a Portuguese accent she introduced herself as Alba. "I cook for the boys." She smiled but then turned back to her work in a way that made me suspect I was intruding. I returned to my room and wondered how long I would have to wait for Massi to awake. Through the window I could see the ocean, where slow waves hunched and tumbled. Restless, I opened a notebook full of messily copied religious verse.

Precious and beautiful flowers we are,
virgins solitary for the love of the Savior.

Difficult Thoughts

And our celibate brothers, married penitents,
remain saintly in this world, to serve the Creator.

It had sounded much better in Italian. Only two months had gone by since I'd begun the project, and already I was forgetting what had drawn me to it in the first place: poetry based on something as pure—and, for me, elusive—as faith. I tried to recall the misty spires and echoing church bells that I had held in mind back when I wrote my proposal. Raised without religion, I had always romanticized the life of the devout. I couldn't abandon them now, these nuns who had spent their lives in pursuit of something so intangible and—to me—uncertain. I looked at a scrawled stanza in my notebook:

Let each of us humble her heart at the sight
of high majesty washing the feet of fishermen.
In God's name, we witness humility:
the most honored one is the most humble of all.

The words lay flat and meaningless on the page. I lifted my head in frustration and saw someone passing my door—a woman with silver hair, clothed in a silk dressing gown. When she turned her face toward me, her eyes stood out like bright chips of blue stone. Taken by surprise, I was unable to speak. Instead I managed a smile, but the woman was already turning away, passing my door slowly but seamlessly, as if propelled by the exhale of a whisper.

It was their mother, I decided, and felt my heart fight between the urge to sink and the will to pound furiously at such insult. How could they not have introduced us, or even mentioned me to her, or her to me? I understood there being no mention of Alba, since she probably didn't live here, but their mother was different. Was I that unimportant to Massi? I decided that I would ignore it and not say anything. Perhaps Massi meant to introduce us today. I would be patient and wait. I looked back at my notebook and read to myself.

The brothers slept until eleven-forty-five and then acted annoyed that by the time we were dressed, fed, and ready to start on the day's excursion it was already afternoon and we would have just a few hours before changing for cocktails and then dinner; we were to meet their friends at a restaurant that night. Now the brothers stood in the foyer trying to decide just which sight they had so wanted to show me. Alba, dragging a vacuum cleaner into the living room, asked where we were going.

Marcello said, "We haven't quite decided," and lit a cigarette to indicate that it was not a question to be easily resolved.

"It's so cold out," Alba said. "Why don't you just stay in and relax."

Marcello's ears seemed to perk at the word "relax." He said, "We could look at photographs."

"Don't be boring," Massi said, and then seemed at a loss. It was then that I noticed a movement out on the balcony, where a drizzle coated the few plants still living. Their mother, in her silk robe and holding a pair of gardening shears, approached a few drooping leaves. Her movements were as slow and smooth as the clouds that moped across the sky beyond her.

I waited for one of the brothers to say something, to wave at her through the glass balcony door, but they had already headed out to the corridor, where Massi was opening the cage of the antique elevator. I stepped into the ornate cubicle and stood there flanked by Marcello and Massi, who appeared worn out by the morning's events. In the mirror beside us was a twenty-eight-year-old woman with a runny nose and two bored bodyguards.

We spent the afternoon shivering at a few deserted ports, the brothers pointing out pleasant views and arguing with each other over who had lost more money at the track. I tried to commit to memory the brightly painted shutters against the white, stifled sky and waited patiently for Massi to secretly stroke my hand or rub my back. I waited for some revelation—of touch, of a whisper. Back in town, we walked silently under the arcades, lowering our heads to the cold air.

At the restaurant, it became evident that I was supposed to be with Marcello. Not that anyone actually said as much, but it was silently understood, the way that the people I met glanced at him with smiles, sent him winks of approval, and left room for me next to him at the bar. After all, here I was, a lone *americana*; it was assumed that I had been procured by one of the brothers, and Massi, I discovered, already had Vittoria. She was a big, bronze girl of about twenty, with violet eyes and straight, shiny brown hair she wore in a bandeau. She sat chain-smoking at the bar and tended to glare at Massi, but with Marcello her gaze was soft. They whispered jokes to each other, Marcello's head falling onto her shoulder, while Vittoria tossed her head back and laughed.

However long Vittoria had been Massi's partner, it was long enough for him to comfortably ignore her. The resigned silence made their relationship seem all the more permanent. I decided to take the same—silent—approach toward Vittoria, but when we sat down to our meal at the long wooden table, I found myself beside her. Marcello, on my left, kept reaching over my plate to poke her with the cutlery.

At Vittoria's right, Massi and some friends discussed the walnut sauce and ways to avoid military service. There were wars going on, just a few borders away, but the conversation suggested no relation between this fact and one's civil duty. Enlistment appeared to be not so much a risk or obligation as an unpleasant waste of time.

I suppose you could say I felt similarly about my abrupt coupledom with Marcello. I remembered Massi's smooth hands in the back seat of the Fiat. It seemed years ago. Now I watched him, oblivious to me, engaged in conversation. A man named Ivo was recounting how he had escaped the military on grounds of poor health.

"That's what I'm going to do," Marcello piped in. "Tell them about my back problem."

Massi looked only slightly concerned. "You have a back problem?"

"I have a pain."

"But, Massi," Ivo cut in, "I don't understand why they want you in Milan. Can't you just join the La Spezia marines? We're practically across the street. You could probably even sleep and eat at home. It would be just the way it always is."

"Well, of course; that's what I've been trying to do. But I have trouble swimming—heavy bones or something—so they're sending me to Milan instead. I told them, though, that I don't need a job where I'm on the water. I have a friend who when he did his military service just washed dishes in the mess hall. I suggested

I would be good at that." Massi squinted his eyes to take a drag on his cigarette. "I'm waiting to hear if they're able to change my assignment."

I looked to see if Vittoria's face might reveal more regarding the situation. Perhaps Massi wanted to get away from her. Or did he truly hope to be posted right here, in town? What was it about Vittoria that could keep him wanting her, besides her violet eyes and prudish hairband? Perhaps I would never know. She reached behind me to pinch Marcello, but he was listening to a joke being told across the table. Dejectedly, Vittoria squeezed a bit of lemon over her fillet. In a moment of solidarity, I turned to her and asked, "What do you think of Massi and Marcello's mother?"

"She never liked me," Vittoria said flatly. "But, then, she never liked anyone."

"But she likes you now?" I asked.

"She's dead," Vittoria said.

"But—" I stopped myself from speaking. "Oh," I said, slowly understanding that the woman I had seen in the apartment was not their mother. She was yet another one of this collection Massi appeared to have, women popping up everywhere, in kitchens, on balconies, in restaurants. I supposed I was one, too. "When did she die?" I asked.

"About two years ago," said Vittoria. "I guess they still don't talk about it much."

"They must miss her," I suggested.

Vittoria raised her brows slightly. "She was an impatient woman, and yet she put up with too much. She didn't know how to handle her husband. She let herself be ignored, and so he pushed her aside until there was nothing left of her." Vittoria poured herself some more wine. "I know how to handle men," she said. "I would never let myself become like that. Still, you have to be patient."

I eyed Massi, who was listening to a curly-haired woman I couldn't remember meeting—yet another one of the menagerie, I guessed. "Or perhaps you could play in the marching band," the woman was saying. "My cousin played the clarinet, and he never had to do any combat drills at all. Do you play an instrument?"

Massi paused thoughtfully before saying, "I used to play the cymbals."

The woman's eyes lit up, and she said, "Well, there you go. They're sure to need a cymbal player."

The conversation continued along these lines until late. By 2 a.m. the restaurant had emptied, and it was just the four of us. Marcello popped the top from a bottle of Bailey's and poured himself a low glass. In what appeared to be a usual pattern, he then said that he wasn't feeling quite well and should like to return home, and Massi decided to stay over at Vittoria's. I looked at Massi's tired face and Vittoria's bright eyes and realized that my one real reason for being in La Spezia no longer existed.

"I have to leave tomorrow," I told Marcello as we walked into the damp night air. All we could hear were the splashes of waves on rock and the click of my heels on stone. "I'm feeling guilty about my work," I explained. "I'll need to take the early train. Please tell Massi I said goodbye."

I boarded the train through the morning's frigid mist, my bag heavy with books and translated texts. To guilt myself into

working, I imagined the cloistered nuns, their life's work abandoned, never to be more than a pile of illegibly bilingual note-
cards. Settling into a seat, I opened my notebook and read:

I have sinned and have offended my Lord.
Thus, for His love, that He may pardon me,
Joyously I scourge my shoulders and belly
To escape the serpent who wants to devour me.

About five miles out of the station, the conductor decided to
fare sciopero. He stopped the train in a misty field, made a brief
speech about workers' rights, and ran away. Through the window
I watched him flee across plots of some tall, dead, unharvested
grain. We waited for a replacement conductor until it became
clear that none was coming. I knew I ought to find a hotel, or
camp out at the station. All around me businessmen made calls
on cellular phones. They had places to be, people to miss them,
family to wonder where they were. Borrowing a phone, I dialed
the brothers' number.

Marcello managed to look pleased at being stuck with a guest he
had just gotten rid of. "It means you're one of the family," he
said. "You should stay awhile."

"I can't," I said, aware of a note of panic in my voice. "You
don't understand. I'm on a grant. I have to do my work."

"What work?" said Marcello innocently. "The nuns? Come
here; let's have a look." I peevishly handed him my notebook.

"Here we go," he said as he opened it. " 'O sorrowful sisters, now give a black mantle / to her who cared neither for beautiful silk nor good veil / For I am so abandoned and widowed by my son.' " Marcello slammed the book shut. "Sounds good to me."

"Widowed by my son," I said out loud. "It moves me, actually." I felt my eyes well up, thinking of what I had been through that summer. Then I stared hard at Marcello and said, "Vittoria told me your mother died."

"Yes," he said, looking down. "Two years ago. My father finally went off with his girlfriend, and my mother never recovered."

"And who is the woman who lives here now?" I asked, with a bit more force.

"Alba doesn't live here," said Marcello.

"I mean the woman with the silver hair. In the silk robe."

Marcello looked at me with surprise, nodded slowly, and said, "So you've seen her."

"Yes, who is she? Why haven't you introduced me?"

"She is my mother," Marcello said. "I can't introduce you because she's dead."

"I don't understand," I told him, surprised at how whiny I sounded. "I don't understand." Then I took a deep breath and said firmly, "I don't believe you."

"Yes, it's problematic," said Marcello. "But I've seen her, too. I don't know what else to tell you."

I just stared at him.

"I understand if that makes you uncomfortable," Marcello continued. "Massi asked a friend of ours—he knows about these things—and he said to ignore her. Only if people notice them do they stay. If you stop paying attention to her, she'll eventually leave." Marcello wrinkled his forehead slightly. "It's true, I think. I don't see much of her any more."

I looked at Marcello, at the resigned slope of his shoulders, and realized that this was probably the most thought he had ever given to the subject. "I have work to do," I said huskily, and went to the leather couch to read for the rest of the morning. "I'm sure the evening train will be back on schedule."

Massi looked happy to find me there on the sofa when he got home that afternoon. I explained about the train, that there would be another one that evening, and found myself looking up at him with the same longing as before. It was just loneliness, really, but I waited for some revelatory gesture, a hand on my back, on my hair. Massi sat down next to me and put his mouth on my neck. In an instant, I felt myself forgiving him for everything, his secrets and mysteries. Massi took me in his arms and moved his mouth toward my ear. "They've changed my assignment," he said, and pulled back to reveal a smile. "I'll be stationed here."

We discussed a vague, dreamy future—from which Vittoria was mysteriously absent—in which I worked in Florence weekdays and visited Massi in La Spezia on weekends, when he was off dishwashing/cymbal duty. Its hopelessness was comforting. But when Massi leaned over to kiss my mouth, I sat up and pushed him away. "I've seen your mother," I said. "In the hallway, and then on the balcony, gardening."

"My mother is dead," Massi said softly, and then seemed to

decide that no explanation was worth the effort. He shrugged his shoulders and said, "If you believe you've seen her, then you've seen her. It's certainly what she wants you to think. People believe what they want to believe."

Though I should have known better, I waited for him to say something else. I still believed he had more to offer. My expectant, curious eyes must have held the same expression that often meets me now, when from a podium in front of a chalkboard I look out into a broad plot of lecture hall. This is at one of the few colleges still reserved for the female sex and therefore unable to shake the appellation of "girls' school"; I stand in front of my Renaissance studies class to see row upon row of budding Vittorias. Some look bored and self-assured, some chew pencil ends or their own hair, some frantically copy my words into notebooks. And some, jaws half open, eyes too patient to blink, watch me with trusting confidence, waiting for some wisdom that I myself am not sure I possess.

What would they think if I told them the truth, that I still, two years later, and for all my lack of explanation, at times see that silver-haired woman with the silk robe—on the winding paths of campus, and in corridors, in doorways, looking lost or staring out a window? It isn't often that she turns up, but with a certain regularity. Sometimes she appears in busy places, waiting in line at the movies, or filling a grocery cart with produce.

That winter in La Spezia, I was sure there was an explanation. I thought that by returning to Florence, to the cold library and my tired notebooks, I could make sense of mystery. I was still of the mind that what was studied could be learned.

And so, when evening arrived and I again said goodbye, I watched for what more the brothers might reveal. Massi just warned me not to study too hard, and Marcello gave me a little package of cough drops and syrup (wrapped in his exam schedule, I later noticed). They waited with me as the elevator creaked up to their floor, and I stepped into the compartment for a last time. Through the gilt bars, I watched Massi bring a lit match to the tip of his cigarette. He looked pensive as ever. "It's a shame you have to go," he said, exhaling. "You really should stay." The smoke from his cigarette wrote some flimsy, short-lived message in the air.

Rehearsal Dinner

"Everything in this car is automatic," Pierre-Luc announced, ushering Geoff into the front passenger's seat. His accent turned it into *otomateek*. "Even the window wipers. They turn on *otomateeklee* when it rains. That's what the man at Hertz said."

His wife, Caroline, slid into the back seat. "It even talks!" she added. "If you leave your keys in the ignition, it tells you to take them out. Things like that. According to the Hertz guy." She had a Toronto inflection that made her sound innocent and somewhat dim.

"Is it male or female?" Geoff had to ask.

"Good question." Pierre-Luc was in the driver's seat now. "We'll have to forget our keys and find out."

Caroline said, "I hope it's a girl."

At the sound of the ignition, Geoff felt the seat belt tighten over his chest. Exhausted, dehydrated, hungry, and still hungover, it was all he could do to make the very smallest of small talk. "Thanks for offering me a ride," he told them. "I appreciate your waiting for me."

"It only makes sense," Caroline said. "Eileen mentioned that your flight was coming in just a bit after ours, and it only made sense."

"And you don't look much in shape for driving," Pierre-Luc added, "if you don't mind my saying so."

Geoff mustered a laugh to match Pierre-Luc's. "Yeah, well, who knows what kind of a lunatic you've just picked up." He had meant to make a joke but immediately regretted trying. At fault was the so-long-we'll-miss-you party thrown by his colleagues (the few remaining ones) yesterday evening; the company he worked for out in Oregon had been bought by a larger corporation, and even though Geoff had weathered two previous rounds of downsizing, in the end all but the top tier of employees had been let go.

It was the fitting conclusion to a generally bad year. Twelve months earlier he and his girlfriend had separated, leaving him alone in a house hexed by her absence.

All year he had struggled to not feel guilty about it. He had stayed away from women, afraid to hurt one, afraid of the serious talks and big decisions that being with one might entail. To feel that strongly about anyone ever again seemed impossible. Even everything he had felt before hadn't been strong enough.

As they swung onto the highway, Pierre-Luc declared, "We have no map."

"Didn't the Hertz guy give you one?" Caroline asked.

"No, but I'm sure we can find it. We'll just point ourselves straight toward the ocean."

They were heading up Boston's North Shore, out to that tiny scenic tip that was Rockport, Massachusetts. There Geoff was to be the Best Man in his childhood best friend's wedding. Tonight he was to attend the rehearsal dinner.

Already it was six, but the September sun was still bright enough to remind Geoff of his headache. He shaded his eyes with his hand. They had driven only a few miles farther when Caroline said, "I have to tinkle."

"This," Pierre-Luc explained without exasperation, "is our pattern. With your permission, I will pull over and allow my dear wife some relief."

Geoff thought they would stop at a rest area, but Pierre-Luc pulled over at the first tree-lined spot, and Caroline didn't seem to think this odd at all. She headed back into the woods with a cheery, "Be right back!"

"Twenty-five years of traveling together," Pierre-Luc said, "you come to expect certain things."

Geoff nodded, and his head gave a little throb-throb. After being out all night with his co-workers, he had gone straight to the airport for a morning departure. Luckily he had packed his suit and gift and shoes and tie the day before. What he had forgotten to do was eat, and the cross-country flight was one of those bargain ones without meals. Geoff had downed two bags of mini-pretzels that did little to soak up the alcohol, while nausea prevented him from drinking anything else. Queasy, hungry, his mouth dry, he hadn't slept at all those six hours. He wondered how he would make it until the rehearsal dinner.

Rehearsal Dinner

"Eileen told us you grew up on the same street with her and Mack. Your folks still live here?"

"Yeah, my mother's in the area." His father and stepmother had recently moved down to North Carolina. "I'm actually moving back here myself."

"What a lucky mother!"

"It's for a job, actually." Geoff had begun sending out his résumé as soon as it became clear he might not be able to hang on to the Portland position much longer.

"Any special girl in your life?"

The question took Geoff off guard. He was used to women making such queries—older women, usually, his relatives or his parents' friends—but not men.

"Not at the moment." Not for a year, he might have added, but he felt too ill.

Pierre-Luc shook his head. "Every man needs a special woman in his life. I firmly believe that. You know why?"

Geoff managed a "Why?"

"Quality of life!" Pierre-Luc cried triumphantly.

Geoff tried to nod, as if understanding.

"They smell good and are kind and can do all sorts of things we can't! Why go through things alone when you can do them with a woman?"

"Right on," Geoff said weakly, sensing that it was his turn to talk.

"Have you ever noticed how much more comfy a woman's bed is than a man's? Have you ever noticed how much better food tastes when a woman makes it? And the best thing is, it only takes one! One wonderful woman!"

Geoff tried to absorb what Pierre-Luc was telling him. You

think it's about love, his mother had scolded, angry at him after his breakup last year. You think it's about love, when really it's about dirty socks.

That alone might have been enough to keep him out of the arena these twelve months. Who needed it? Dirty socks.

"I've been with Caroline since I was twenty-eight," Pierre-Luc told him. "Three times she has tried to kill me. Not maliciously—just in a passionate rage. She's that type. Emotional. You wouldn't know it, but she's full of surprises. That's the secret."

Geoff had heard this sort of thing before, "the secret" to a happy marriage, to a healthy relationship, to a satisfying sex life. But there couldn't be just one secret; Geoff had been given all kinds of advice and none of it matched up. There was his mother and the dirty socks, and his grandfather saying, Just pretend you can't hear, and that mystic who read tarot cards at a restaurant he sometimes went to who had, without Geoff's having asked, told him one Thursday, a few weeks ago now, "Give your love away. Find the love within you and send it out." He had spied on couples he thought of as perfect together—the ones who seemed like equals, who laughed and kissed a lot. Ones like Callie and Mack, getting married tomorrow, who when they were together, easy and relaxed, made it look perfectly simple. But how simple could it be, when they had broken up at least three times? And yet something had kept them coming back to each other. That was the part that Geoff envied: the force that told them to go back to each other, a force he had never known. He wondered what it must feel like—that sureness, real or imagined, that what they were doing was right.

"Thanks, guys." Caroline was back, fresh-faced. "We'd better get a move on if we're going to get there on time."

"Notice how she says this as if I've pulled over for no good reason. As if our sitting and chatting has nothing to do with a certain someone's petite and charming bladder."

Caroline reached over and clunked Pierre-Luc lightly on the head. "Let's go, buster."

Pierre-Luc pulled onto the highway, and Geoff leaned back into the headrest. He knew he should be composing his toast for tomorrow night, but he kept drifting off into something that wasn't quite sleep. It was more like hallucination: a large soda floating in front of him, taunting him. This, he realized, was what he wanted more than anything right now. One of those big vats they give you at the movies, more like a tub, something you might wash your feet in. Sweet and bubbly and full of caffeine.

"I'm hungry," Caroline said.

Geoff sat up straighter, though he supposed this was merely a mirage, or wishful thinking.

"And we arrive," said Pierre-Luc, "at stage two of our travel sequence."

"Just a little something to tide me over," Caroline said. "I can eat in the car. That okay with you, Geoff?"

"My wife has a very fast metabolism," Pierre-Luc told him. "This means that we've been accorded familiarity with every fast food joint along every highway here and in Canada."

Geoff, elated, said, "I could use a soda and maybe even a burger myself."

Within a minute they were at a drive-through, only two cars in line in front of them. Geoff breathed the sweet, sticky smell of processed food, a wave of thick air rushing over him. He thought he might faint from longing.

"That's funny," Pierre-Luc said. "I can't seem to roll down the window."

"Did you try pushing the button?"

"I can't find the button." He was pushing little buttons all along his door, and then began fiddling with the dashboard. The dashboard lights came on and then went off again. "*Cibolaque*. I thought they said everything was *otomateek*."

Geoff's head was swimming now, from the thick scent of oil and sugar and meat seeping in through the completely sealed car. "Maybe we're supposed to talk to it?" he suggested, desperate now. "Didn't the car rental guy say it was voice-activated?"

"I think it was the other way around," Caroline said, but then tried, experimentally, to issue a command. In a soft, diffident voice, she said, "Please open the windows."

They waited, expectantly.

Caroline said, "Pretty please?"

"Open the windows!" Pierre-Luc tried, grandly, before grumbling "*cibolaque*" and going back to flicking levers and turning knobs.

Geoff felt his stomach gulp the greasy air. He screamed: "Open the goddamn windows!"

At that, the horn shouted out—and continued to yelp, over and over, a quick yet steady cry of alarm. "Now, how did I set that off?" Pierre-Luc asked, as the passengers in the car ahead of them turned to see what the trouble was.

"Refill window washer fluid."

"Who the hell was that?" he asked.

"Refill window washer fluid."

Caroline said, "Aw, it's a girl after all."

Rehearsal Dinner

Geoff tried to laugh, but his own exertion, and the thick aroma of hamburgers and soda, and the hammering horn and the lights flashing on the dashboard, had weakened him completely. His seat belt tightened suddenly around him.

"Replace oil filter."

Caroline said, "My goodness, she's getting demanding."

"A door is ajar. Replace oil filter. Refill window washer fluid. Check oil. A door is ajar."

The horn, too, continued to complain, and now the windshield wipers joined in, waving in panic. Geoff's head felt as though it might crack, as though it were already cracking, from the base above his neck up to the very top of his skull.

"Refill your self."

Geoff tried to unsquint his eyes, as if that would help him hear better.

"Fulfill your heart."

He looked to Pierre-Luc, who was examining the steering wheel, saying, "Now, I wonder what this thing does." Caroline was again speaking politely to the window, asking it to please open.

"Find her. Love her."

In a sweat, Geoff swung his head around, to see where the voice was coming from. The windshield wipers flapped frantically back and forth. "Don't wait any longer. Remake your life. Don't wait any lon—"

With an abrupt sigh, the car shut itself off completely. The horn stopped mid-honk, the lights flashed one last time, and the wipers froze in action, splayed across the glass. Geoff exhaled deeply.

"Well, now, that did something," Pierre-Luc said with satisfaction, as the car in front of them drove off. "Do I dare turn this thing on again?"

Geoff was trying to catch his breath.

"We're up," Caroline said.

Pierre-Luc flipped the ignition, and the engine made an encouraging sound.

Without any coaxing, all of the windows slid down.

"How fortunate," Caroline said, as if used to such occurrences. Pierre-Luc drove forward a few feet to the intercom.

Geoff's heart was still pounding, and he wondered how these two people could remain so unflustered. It was as if they were used to confusion, to turmoil, as if they accepted it fully and without worry. They hadn't yelled at each other. They hadn't panicked. Caroline hadn't scolded Pierre-Luc the way Geoff's mother would have done to his father back when they were still together. And yet, from what Pierre-Luc had said—well, if Caroline really had tried to kill her husband, then surely a temperamental car was nothing to them.

But he couldn't deny what he himself had heard. Could they tell? Did he look as insane as he felt? He was afraid to open his mouth, afraid of what he might say. But he managed to blurt out his order, and the next thing he knew, a hamburger and soda were being handed to him. He ate in gulps and took long swills from his drink, barely chewing his food. Soon he felt sated as he never had before.

He closed his eyes. He must have slept, because when he next opened them the sun was setting, and the road had narrowed to two lanes without becoming particularly scenic. Though Geoff didn't remember dreaming, he felt he had been somewhere; a sensation of strong, if unclear, conviction ran

Rehearsal Dinner

through him. He tried to recall a story line or image but came up with nothing. Stretching his arms, he turned to see the bright ball of sun as it dropped onto the horizon.

"I have to tinkle."

Pierre-Luc was pulling over to the shoulder now. Geoff looked out at the trees, the usual side-of-the-road type, nothing especially lush or promising about them. But they stood nobly, and Geoff was gripped by a sudden and precise certainty—that someone was out there for him, and that, when the time came, he would know exactly what to do.

Calamity

They had been in the air for less than an hour when Rhea heard a popping sound. It seemed to come from outside, maybe from one of the wings, and though it wasn't anything Rhea had ever heard before, she knew instinctively that it was a bad sound.

"Did you hear that?" said the woman in the next seat.

Rhea said no.

"You didn't hear that?"

"No."

Rhea said no partly because she found denial a perfectly acceptable way of preventing panic, and partly because she did not like—again, instinctively—this woman, who, as a standby passenger, had claimed seat 36B at the very last minute, just when Rhea had confidently placed her bag there and arranged

along both tray tables the folder full of student papers she suspected she would not read, the magazine she knew she would,
and the little leather journal in which she recorded tersely
phrased personal insights. Then came this big woman, too
much of her for her seat, with coarse dark hair and a broad
shock of white on top, like a skunk. She looked to be a good
forty years older than Rhea, seventy or so, and wore enormous
eyeglasses that wove in gold across the bridge of her nose. The
air immediately filled with the too-sweet smell of imitation
perfume—probably, Rhea thought to herself, something in
misspelled French. The glasses were real, Christian Dior—
printed on the outer part of the left temple, another horizon-
tal gold braid.

It was at that point, after gathering back her belongings, that
Rhea had written in her little notebook, "I am living proof that it
does not take money to be a snob."

From the way the woman wedged herself into her seat with
an unrestrained wheeze, her long flowered skirt catching on the
armrest, Rhea knew that she was one of those people who had no
trouble falling asleep in public places, drooling even, sprawling
out on bus seats and in movie theaters. And, true to form, the
woman had even snored a little, while Rhea skimmed an article
entitled "Turn Him On—with Minimal Makeup!"

"There, did you hear that?" the woman asked again.

"Hear what?"

But it was no good lying anymore, because just then the
plane took a sudden dip and, just as quickly, righted itself.

Around them, people murmured nervously.

"Oh my God," said the woman. "You can't say you didn't feel
that."

"Fine, you're right." Rhea blamed the woman for forcing her to admit it. "Happy now?"

The woman turned to stare at Rhea, enormous glasses magnifying her dark eyes. Rhea too was shocked at her outburst. She attributed it to fear—of the plane's odd behavior, and of the coming weekend in Massachusetts, yet another event she preferred not to think about. She wished she had taken advantage of the airport bar before boarding. There had certainly been time enough, two hours of delay due to technical problems with the plane, which Rhea now considered mentioning to the standby woman, who had conveniently missed that whole chapter of the experience.

The captain's voice, a lazy-sounding one, came at them:

"Folks. It appears we're having some problems with our right hydraulic system. What that means is that, rather than continue on to Logan, we're going to have to land at the closest runway, which is in Baltimore. I've just spoken with the folks at BWI, and it looks like they can clear us for landing in about twenty minutes. So, if you'll bear with us. We apologize for the inconvenience."

"Inconvenience?" said the standby woman. She sounded like she might be from New Jersey. "Landing without a right hydraulic system." She shook her head. "Well, I'm sure he'll do a fine job. Even without the right hydraulic system. I'm sure he's a fine pilot."

Rhea said, "It doesn't matter if he's fine or not." She hadn't mean to snap. But the plane was veering a little to the right, now back to the left, and now made another sudden, brief plunge.

The woman took a short, frightened breath. Her perfume seemed momentarily stronger.

Calamity

161

"He's probably testing the plane," Rhea told the standby woman, wishing it were true. "Seeing which functions are still working."

"It's my fault," said the standby woman.

"What's your fault?"

"I'm bad luck. Nothing ever goes smoothly when I'm involved. If I'm in a car, there's a flat tire. Or a traffic jam. If I go to a movie, there's some black thing flickering on the screen. If you invite me to a wedding, it rains."

Rhea thought for a moment and said, "That's incredibly egotistical."

The standby woman did not seem to have heard her. "I'm a jinx."

"Everyone thinks that about themselves," said Rhea.

"But with me it's true," said the standby woman.

"Believe me. It isn't. I know for certain. None of this is your fault."

"How do you know?"

Rhea knew because it was *her* fault. This fact had become suddenly clear to her. For months she had been dreading Callie and Mack's wedding, regretted ever having agreed to be Maid of Honor. Never mind the inconvenience of it, with the semester barely started and Rhea only a month into her new job. Never mind that the flight from Virginia, where she had accepted a professorship at a small private college, had cost enough to make her regret ever having moved there in the first place. That wasn't the half of it—and yet Rhea had said yes. After all, Callie was her oldest childhood friend, and had asked her without—

Rhea could not even allow herself to continue the thought. Each day that the wedding drew closer, Rhea had waited for some

Calamity

emergency to present itself, something that might prevent her from attending. If only a problem arose that was completely out of her control, then she would have an excuse.

The plane tilted oddly back, as if stretching its head to yawn.

Around them, people were making panicky sounds.

"You see?" said the standby woman. "I'm bad luck."

"Fine!" Rhea said. "Blame it on her, everyone. She's the cause of all this." It came out more loudly than Rhea had intended.

The woman turned toward her, gigantic lenses for eyes, looking stunned. The plane tilted forward, and then more forward. Rhea gripped her armrests. More general panic was expressed before the structure found its balance.

The woman's eyes had welled with tears. She sniffed into the little square napkin that had come with her complimentary beverage, and reached behind the enormous gold frames to dab at her eyes.

"See that?" said Rhea. "You thought things were bad, and now you see that it wasn't so bad after all. So what if the right hydraulic system failed. Maybe it's worse to have your neighbor saying mean things to you, making a spectacle of the both of us."

"I'm glad you're able to see that."

"Look at the bright side. We're heading to the airport, and the plane's still, miraculously, in the air. Be thankful. Be glad."

"Okay, I will," said the woman.

"Because I'll tell you something," Rhea continued. "No matter how bad it gets, it can always get worse."

As if to confirm this, the captain came on the intercom and said, "Well, folks. It looks like we're having some trouble with our front wing flaps."

Nervous groans came from all around, the intonation of whiny question marks.

"What this means," the pilot went on, "is that our landing is going to be more difficult than anticipated. We do still have full brake control, but we are going to have to instruct you in the proper emergency landing procedure. So I'd like you to please give your full attention to Irene and Nat, who in a few minutes will provide detailed instructions."

"See that?" said Rhea.

"Oh God," said the woman.

"And you know what?" Rhea went on, unsure of what exactly propelled her. "Even now, it could still get worse."

"What, do you want it to?" The woman gave a huff.

"I'm just trying to put it in perspective. This is not at all as bad as all kinds of terrible things. You know what I read in the paper the other day? I read about a guy, some young father here in the good old U.S. of A., who went out with a buddy of his and left his baby daughter in the car, windows rolled up, on a sunny ninety-degree day. Just left her there while he and his friend went fishing or something."

"That's horrible," said the standby woman, and added, tentatively, "Did she die?"

"Of course," Rhea told her. "But that wasn't the worst part. When they came back to the car, the baby had been so hot and miserable, she had torn her hair out of her head."

"Oh my God."

"A little baby with fists full of her own hair." Rhea took a breath. "So you see, we don't have it so bad."

The woman said, "I can't believe you just told me that."

"I'm sorry," Rhea said. "Talking makes me feel better. I like to put things in perspective."

Actually, Rhea suspected that her habit of putting things in perspective was the very problem with the way she lived her life. To be so aware, constantly aware, of the many horrors in the world made it hard to take your own problems seriously. And yet it was no help, Rhea knew, to belittle her own existence. That hadn't made it any less painful when her fiancé left her, or when she didn't get the Tufts job, or when a journal rejected a paper of hers. If only she could shake that greater pessimism—that resigned acceptance of life's constant abominations—that she so often let guide her decisions. She had given so many things up that way, and betrayed Callie with the same reasoning. That persistent reminder, the threat of calamity, had allowed her to justify all kinds of actions she now regretted.

Rhea opened up her little leather-bound notebook and wrote neatly, "Hypothetical life is always better."

The captain asked them to please give their attention to Nat and Irene.

Rhea thought for a moment and said aloud, "Don't women ever get to be captains?"

The standby woman took only a moment before saying, "No, no, I don't think so."

Rhea nodded, mystery solved. That was what Rhea liked about older women. You could count on them for the truth, because they had lived it. Young people pretended that the world was better than it had once been, because that was what should be true. Older women could state the actual reality—the limitations and injustices that prevailed—because they had grown up in a world where these things were said outright.

Rhea opened her little notebook again and wrote, "Old women are good for the facts."

Nat and Irene had begun their performance. On a broad screen glowed a detailed accompanying video. Rhea focused her attention on Irene, who stood closest and, with hair in a stiff ponytail, told her audience that they would need to remove all jewelry, eyewear, headwear, hair clips, and false teeth.

Even though Rhea knew that what she was being told might save her life, the old student in her had dredged up from her school days a natural resistance to instruction, so that she found it impossible, even now, to give Irene her full, respectful concentration. Instead, she found herself wondering who would pick her up at Logan. "Don't worry, someone will come get you," Callie had said in her easy way. But what if it were Mack? Would Rhea be able to keep from telling him? Would she be able to not cry? And then Rhea remembered that she might not make it to the airport.

Irene was now demonstrating how to crouch in the proper position, head between knees, hands grasped behind the neck. She asked the passengers to please practice this position, and Rhea bent forward. The position was not comfortable. She sat up, as others had.

Irene instructed them to please practice this position again.

She's just saying that to kill time, thought Rhea. But, like an obedient child, she bent over again.

The standby woman was too big to do this properly. Giving up, she said to Rhea, "I used to be thin, like you. On my wedding day I weighed ninety-nine pounds."

Is that some sort of threat? Rhea wanted to ask. No, she thought, just another musing on loss, now that tragedy seemed imminent.

The captain spoke. "Folks. We have not yet been cleared for landing." There was the pause of the intercom clicking off, then on again. "It looks like we're going to have to circle for about ten more minutes. Thank you for your patience."

The flight attendants were making their way down the aisles, checking that everyone was following the proper procedure.

"I suppose I should introduce myself," the woman said. "I'm Gaylord."

Rhea thought to herself how many times this poor woman had said that name and watched people act like it was perfectly acceptable. Except for when she was in elementary school, thought Rhea. I bet she was teased a lot.

"My name's Rhea."

In elementary school they had called her Dia Rhea.

Gaylord said, "I'm going to visit my son. He has two boys. I haven't seen them in a few months. Not since my husband's funeral. I'm a new widow."

She said "new widow," Rhea thought, the way one might say "recent graduate" or "nouveau riche." Well, maybe she was newly rich, buying whatever she could off of her husband's insurance policy. That, come to think of it, might explain the showy eyeglasses.

Some rows ahead of them, a woman was refusing to remove her jewelry. A stewardess could be heard insisting in reasonable, businesslike inflections.

"This was my grandmother's necklace, and I will not take it off."

"Good for her," said Gaylord, carefully folding her glasses into a case of purple leather, which she now clicked shut.

Amazing, thought Rhea, seeing Gaylord's face exposed, puffy pockets of darkened skin under her eyes, little lines all over, her expression sad and overwhelmed, as if she had been suddenly asked to shave her head or walk naked in public. Without her glasses, she no longer looked at all appalling. She did still look a little skunky. Rhea watched as she took from her purse, also purple leather, a gold makeup compact, which she sprung open and peered into with a sigh. With a tiny brush, she applied pale green powder to her eyelids. Then she dabbed a different little brush into some red gel, which she swiped back and forth over her lips.

Primping for death, thought Rhea. Gaylord peeked at herself in the mirror one more time and said, "I look dreadful."

And Rhea thought to herself that they all were, really were, everyone on the aircraft, full of dread.

"If we live through this," she said, though she hadn't meant to put it that way, "do you know what this whole experience will become?"

Gaylord shook her head.

"An anecdote." Rhea knew that the sick feeling that they all had in their stomachs right now would not even return in the telling. It would be recalled and described but not felt.

Gaylord said, "We're going to die together."

"I cannot believe you just said that. Will you please not say that? Really. Do not say that again." Rhea could hear the annoyance in her voice. "You may feel you've lived a full life, but I'm not finished yet, all right?"

Calamity

"I apologize," said Gaylord, sighing.

Behind them, a baby began to wail. All around was the snapping sound of rings, chains, and watches being placed in purses, sunglasses removed and folded.

Rhea opened up her little leather notebook. In all caps she wrote "REGRETS" and underneath, in lowercase, "Do I have any?"

She sat and thought.

"Well, do you?" asked Gaylord.

"Do I what?"

"Have any regrets?"

"You're peeking!"

"So—do you?"

Rhea considered saying, "I regret not having flown first class." But instead she found herself nodding. "Yes." Before she could lose track of her thought, she wrote in her notebook, "I regret having spent the majority of my life trying not to offend others."

Gaylord raised her eyebrows and said, "Could have fooled me."

"You're still spying!"

"What do you expect?"

"See, that's what I mean." What she meant was that Gaylord, unlike herself, dared to tell the truth. She had dared to admit she was looking over Rhea's shoulder. Rhea rarely felt comfortable admitting what she was thinking. "I always try to keep my mouth zipped," she told Gaylord, "I try to hide my true thoughts, but they always seem to pop out. And then I feel rude, when I say what I think. It's just nerves today, freeing me up that way. And I resent that. I resent that it takes an emergency landing for me to really say what's what. It's only now that I see I've lived my life trying to be polite."

"But why would you want to be impolite? What good is there in that?"

"I've just spent so much time holding my knees closed, you know? Clasping my hands on my lap. What good does that do the world? I've spent so much time and effort on trying to dress the right way, trying to say the appropriate things. Trying to fit in rather than be a person who accomplishes anything. That's my regret."

Gaylord seemed to be thinking this over. She said, "In other words, you regret having been a woman."

This fact had not occurred to Rhea before, not in those precise words. But now she saw that it was true. "Yes, I regret not having been a man in this world."

She thought of this now, and, returning to the memory she so often arrived at, asked Gaylord, "Any secrets you'll be taking to your grave?"

"What do you mean?"

"Maybe I'm just thinking aloud. Wondering if I have a secret I'd rather die than tell."

"Do you?"

"I have a secret. But I'd rather tell it than die." And it suddenly seemed that she alone could save the airplane, that if she told just one person, they would all be saved. This feeling was overwhelming. She whispered to Gaylord, "When I was twenty-eight I had an abortion."

Gaylord nodded her head and said, "When I was twenty-eight I had a miscarriage."

Calamity

"An abortion is different," said Rhea, annoyed. "And any-way, that's not the whole secret."

Maybe, thought Rhea, Gaylord was one of those religious ladies who stand outside the clinics on weekends, holding rosary beads and photographs of bloody fetuses. But no, Gaylord with her bright stripe of hair simply wouldn't fit in with those tedious, pale women. That shock of white. It suddenly struck Rhea as an incredibly bold thing, to enter the world each day with hair like that.

"So what's the story?" Gaylord asked.

"It was two years ago. I'd known I was pregnant for nearly two months," Rhea told her. "I went through everything you probably did, morning sickness, everything. But I had been awarded a travel grant, a research scholarship, actually, and I was supposed to leave in a few months, and I knew there was no way I could have a baby and go traipsing around Italy. And the father—he. Wasn't my boyfriend. He was my friend's boyfriend."

She paused to bite her upper lip. "I finally convinced myself that everything would be better once I ended the pregnancy. So I didn't tell anyone, and I went to have the abortion and felt completely prepared. Completely ready. And I got there and they did the final checkup beforehand, and you know what? There were two. I was carrying twins."

Rhea felt herself about to cry, but the voice of the head flight attendant came from the intercom. "We will now complete our descent. Please take your positions. We remind you that you are to have removed all headwear, eyewear, jewelry, dentures, retainers, and studs. Please take your positions."

The air swelled with the eerie quiet of controlled panic. Only the screaming baby continued to complain. People spoke in whispery tones as they bent forward, heads between knees, and grabbed their necks.

"I guess this is it," said Gaylord, whose face wasn't quite between her knees.

"What about you?" Rhea asked, head down, voice muffled.

"What about me?"

"What's your secret?"

Gaylord said, "I'm still wearing my false teeth."

Rhea laughed.

"I look bad enough without my glasses. If I die I'm going to at least have my teeth in."

"Top or bottom?"

"Bottom. I look ancient with my jaw all sunken in."

"Accident?"

Gaylord sighed. "My husband."

"Oh!"

"I guess that's my secret."

The captain came on. "Flight attendants, prepare for landing."

Gaylord said, "I started gaining a lot of weight after my first child," as if in explanation.

That was when the plane began heading swiftly toward the ground. No one dared to sigh or squirm. Even the baby stopped screaming. Rhea gripped her neck as tightly as she was able. Down, down, they went, and went, and went, and then hit the ground with incredible force. There was another popping noise, and the plane continued forward at great speed. But it was still in one piece, thought Rhea, at least it seemed to be, unless they were about to slam into something. Rhea supposed that was entirely possible. But then the plane began to slow. Rhea could feel it. They could all feel it, and the air itself seemed to relax, to refill with a collective exhalation.

Gaylord said, "I think we may actually be okay."

Are you trying to jinx it? thought Rhea. But right then the plane came to a stop.

Without waiting for word from the captain, everyone sat up. Above them, oxygen masks dangled like piñatas. They must have been released on impact. Looking out the window, Rhea saw an array of emergency vehicles—fire trucks, ambulances, lights and neon colors. Nat the flight attendant was already making his way down the aisle, explaining that they should not use the oxygen masks.

"They're just for dramatic effect," said Rhea. Indeed, there was an odd air of festival, the hanging masks all around them.

Over the intercom, the captain stated that they were going to have to evacuate the plane via emergency chute. "Please leave all belongings on the plane," he said. "Do not take your belongings with you down the chute. Follow the flight attendants, and leave your belongings on the plane."

All around, women grabbed their pocketbooks. Gaylord had already put her glasses back on. Now she snapped her earrings into place. Her hands were shaking. "I can't believe we made it," she said. Rhea realized that her own hands were trembling.

The emergency exit had been opened, and from outside came the whine of a siren. It really was unnecessary, thought Rhea. But the siren continued as, row by row, passengers stood up to shimmy out of their seats, ducking through the vines of oxygen masks. It was already Rhea and Gaylord's turn. As they waited in the aisle, shaky-legged, Rhea looked at Gaylord, at her astounding glasses and heavy earrings and bright makeup.

"What your husband did to you," said Rhea. "It has nothing to do with your weight. You know that, right?"

Gaylord looked at her in a way that suggested she just barely knew this. But she nodded as Rhea said, "What I mean is—"

Gaylord said, "I know. It was just violence."

As they moved up toward the exit, the siren became louder. *Just violence.* That those words should be allowed side by side . . . Rhea glanced at Gaylord and did not want to imagine her past. The situations people found themselves in on any day, Rhea reflected, were really no less absurd than the one she was in right now, standing here like a third-grader, about to go down a giant inflated slide. I must note this, Rhea thought to herself, and then realized that she no longer had her little leather book. She had left it back at her seat.

"Wait till I tell my grandkids about this slide," Gaylord said, looking truly pleased. "Whoever would have thought I'd be given the chance to go down a slide again?"

The slide really was quite something, enormous and bouncy and neon yellow. Some people hesitated before jumping out. Women kept smuggling their purses along with them.

Rhea said, "Are we really going down that thing?" The airplane itself, improbability incarnate, suddenly seemed safer than that clownish slide. Gaylord did not appear at all worried. She took the flight attendant's hand and then let go. Rhea watched her slide fearlessly down, her skirt hitching up to her waist. With clenched fists, Rhea stepped out to follow her into the world of sirens and lights.

Calamity

Wedding at Rockport

The Maid of Honor was a disgrace. Everyone said so. A delayed flight had delivered her too late to fulfill any of her duties and with much of her luggage lost, so that she was wearing not the proper dress but a slinky blue thing of Indian silk, with many tiny bells hanging from the hem. She had jingled the entire way down the aisle—a clearing of grass that led to a rocky bluff—and the unnerving sound, recurring with each intermittent breeze, made the guests glance away. Now that the ceremony had ended, she was telling everyone about an emergency landing and how her nerves were still shaken—but she had been saying this since the morning, so that now it just seemed like an excuse to drink too much.

"And they say this is a dry town," Annie, a guest on the

groom's side, commented to her best friend, the groom's mother, Eileen. They eyed the Maid of Honor and sipped white wine. Cocktail hour, for which the bride's family had paid a pretty penny, was coming to a close. In fact, it was a half hour only, since the caterers claimed the town's dry status made alcohol—at private engagements only—that much more expensive. Guests milled about the majestic patio and looked out at the sun-and-windswept ocean. The water was rough today. "The girl jingles every time she moves," Annie added, even though she knew perfectly well that Eileen—whom she had known for four decades—wished her son would have married the Maid of Honor instead.

Not that there was anything wrong with the bride. She was a tall, blonde beauty with glowing skin and a generous disposition. "Quite a catch," everyone called her. She had been a swimmer back in high school and still had the body, strong in a buxom, shapely way. For the wedding today she wore no jewelry or veil, just a fitted white dress that showed off her figure. From the right angle, in the late-afternoon sunlight, you could see her underpants through it.

Eileen held nothing against her new daughter-in-law, who was bright in a way that had more to do with mood than intellect. The problem was that Eileen's son needed someone to be hard on him; men were so rarely hard on themselves. He needed someone like the Maid of Honor, who, with her wide, questioning eyes and unruly bob of dark hair, had, everyone knew, nearly won his heart a few years back. Eileen had sensed the energy rather than ease, the storm rather than calm, that stirred within her. Her son needed someone like that. Someone to force him into a role to play, a position to fulfill. Keep him from sliding into disuse.

Watching waves tumble headlong, Eileen hugged herself against a gust of salty air. She had always been extremely thin, and today it was a blessing; there was less of her to brim with emotion, less of her own tongue to bite. Abnegation was precisely what these occasions so often required. Here they all were, an assortment of travel-wearied people thrown together at some inconvenient date, but Eileen could float along. A decade ago, when she was in her fifties, an alarmed doctor told her that because she was so skinny her constitution was nearly 70 percent water. When she asked him what that meant, the doctor looked momentarily stumped before saying, "Nothing."

The wind rustled Eileen's shantung skirt-suit, which the bride's mother had talked her into buying (since it matched nicely her short gray hair and made her eyes look bright). "Just look at that," she said in her ex-smoker's whisper to Annie, admiring the majestic structure hosting them, a Georgian mansion overlooking the ocean. Its broad, ornate widow's walk had been featured prominently in three movies. "Can't you picture some worried fisherman's wife pacing back and forth up there, looking longingly out to sea?" Eileen was herself a widow and could imagine it easily.

Annie said, "I doubt any fisherman's wife ever lived in such a swank joint."

"What about rich ship captains? Someone in whaling."

This former fishing village, where men once risked their lives for mackerel and cod, now flexed its dimples for daytrippers browsing boutiques and art galleries. No sign of the rough existence that put it on a map. Inside the mansion's parlor hung a seascape by Fitz Hugh Lane: Gloucester Harbor posing serenely in warm, comforting colors.

Now they were being ushered by caterers in white bow ties toward the big, rustling tent. Annie and Eileen followed the small crowd past trees with leaves blown backward like dogs' ears. It was a shame about the weather, suddenly cool, with occasional clouds slipping in and out, so that the magnificent sun kept dipping away and then back, on what should have been a warm September day. Abandoned wedding programs—listing sonnets by E. B. Browning and W. Shakespeare next to the names of various bridesmaids—kept blowing across the lawn. And yet everyone said, "You couldn't have asked for better weather!" as if to convince themselves it was true.

In front of the tent was a table dotted with place cards, each listing a guest's name and a Cape Ann geographic location. Behind the table an usher stood making sure none of the cards blew away. Annie located her card and flipped it over eagerly, as if it were a lottery ticket. "Did you get Magnolia? Tell me you got Magnolia."

Eileen had wanted to sit at Salt Island with her friends the Colliers, who were sure to tell bawdy jokes and perhaps even break out in song, but status had indeed placed her at Magnolia, where the bride's parents were already seated.

The table was laid with thick linen and oversized silver cutlery. In the center was a bushy cluster of tall flowers so colorful and healthy they seemed embalmed. The bride's father, Tom, who was a good bit older than his wife and was trying to catch the attention of a caterer, had to lean to the side in order to see around them. He waved to a server and asked for more wine.

Next to him was a wheelchair, and in it his ancient mother-in-law, whom most of the guests had given up trying to chat with, since she didn't hear well. "It's a shame she doesn't do something about her hair," the old woman was saying now, referring to Eileen, who was walking toward them and, with no makeup and that wispy figure, even in silver shantung managed to look—Annie had already told her outright—like an underfed prison inmate.

But Eileen couldn't help glancing toward Folly Cove, two tables away, where the Best Man stood joking with some ushers and their dates. Ten, fifteen, years ago she had seen him on an almost daily basis, he and her son spent so much time together. After he went out to the West Coast, she didn't see him for years, and now here he was again, a man, thirty years old, suddenly somehow transformed. Funny, she thought, how people drift in and out of your life like waves, large and smaller and then suddenly larger again.

"Hello, there!" Annie, ahead of her, was smiling down at the bride's family. Finding her seat, she exclaimed, "What enormous flowers!"

In a crumbling old voice, the grandmother said, "There is fruit hanging from your ears."

Annie's large earrings, caught slightly in the graying frizz of her hair, dangled happily: from the right earlobe, bananas; on the left, a cluster of grapes. She wore a red skirt with black and white polka dots, and a white blouse with a collar of red and black stripes. She told the grandmother, "I've never been a big fan of vegetables."

In her hollowed voice, Eileen said, "At last the party can begin!" Taking her seat, she felt the slightly rough rub of silk shantung. When, a full five months ago, she had stepped out of the Lord & Taylor dressing room, Helen, the bride's mother, had told her, "Oh, it's you, it's absolutely you," and then set about looking for her own suit of shantung, so that the two of them would match. Helen's was gold and showed off her fair skin, so that she nearly sparkled, with her shimmery lipstick, twinkling eyes, and frosted hair. Every time someone complimented her, Helen said, "To tell you the truth, I never even would have looked at it if Eileen hadn't found that silver one. I mean, usually it's the mother of the bride who's supposed to choose her dress first, but Eileen just looked so stunning in that silver one, I had to let her set the tone." Eileen had heard this for hours now, so that the silver suit was starting to feel like a badge of selfishness; she was a woman who hadn't even let the mother of the bride choose her own dress.

Now she said, "Heck, we survived the ceremony."

Helen said, "I had a stash of Kleenex, just in case."

"I had to work to keep her mind off things all morning, let me tell you," her husband put in.

Helen agreed. "We took a beautiful walk down to the end of Bearskin Neck. They have such nice shops there. Have you had a chance to explore a bit?"

"This morning some friends and I went on a whale watch," Eileen offered, though they hadn't seen any whales, just a young pregnant girl vomiting over the prow. The brief drive to Gloucester had been beautiful, with nearby detours to anything that Pierre-Luc's guidebook had allotted a star. They saw Beauport and Hammond Castle and the memorial to all the Gloucester fishermen who had gone "down to the sea in ships"—over ten thousand of them lost at sea, the guidebook said. At Norman's

Woe, Pierre-Luc, reading from his Blue Guide, had quoted Longfellow:

"It was the schooner Hesperus,
  That sailed the wintry sea;
  And the skipper had taken his little daughter,
  To bear him company. . . ."

It really was an awful poem. Eileen at least found comic relief in Pierre-Luc's Québecois accent as he read it:

"Come hidDER! come hidDER! my leedle dudDER,
  And do nut dremble so;
  For I can wedDER de roughest gale
  Dat ever wind did blow."

Helen exclaimed, "Oh, here they come!"

The Best Man had taken the microphone to announce, "Ladies and gentlemen, please put your hands together for Callie and Mack—the new Mr. and Mrs. Rivlin!"

People leaned right and left around the gigantic flowers to glimpse the bride and groom.

"She's taking Mack's name?" Annie asked, clapping.

The grandmother said, "Why wouldn't she?"

"After everything we fought for." Annie gave a sigh but kept clapping. Her attention was drawn to Folly Cove, where one of the ushers had stood up and was shouting, "Speech! Speech!" in the bellowing voice of a fraternity brother. Annie had to shake her head at the fact that men—the species—simply hadn't, as far as she could tell, changed a bit. Next to him, the bride's brother whistled a catcall, and the bride and groom stepped onto the dance floor.

Annie thought to herself, Men really can be awful.

One had given her, for her fifty-fifth birthday, a bottle of white truffle oil that, it turned out, his former wife had given *him* for *his* birthday a year earlier.

The bride's brother whistled again.

One had said, "What's that?" and pointed at Annie's puckered thighs. Until that day—a good fifteen years ago now—Annie had believed cellulite to be a creation of the cosmetics industry. Now it existed, and was part of her own body, all because some man had pointed it out.

The couple began dancing to Duke Ellington. Furrowing her brow, the grandmother asked her son-in-law, "Isn't the bride supposed to dance the first dance with her father?"

Tom said, "Good question." He couldn't quite see over the flower arrangement. After straining for a moment, he picked the entire thing up, spilling some water on the table, and placed it on the ground behind his chair. "I don't get the sense they're necessarily following all the traditions," he said good-naturedly.

"If that's the case," Annie said, "why did they go ahead and have the quartet play that boring Canon in D just like the rest of the universe?"

Eileen elbowed Annie, and Tom, who had paid for the quartet, gave a genial shrug. The caterers had begun making their rounds, doling out roasted vegetables and filet mignon on porcelain plates, each slab of meat topped with a little floret of butter. The servers were still at the far left side of the tent, so that everyone toward the right felt suddenly hungry, realizing how long it would be until they were served. There was hushed talk about buffets and the many benefits of having no sit-down meal at all. The Best Man announced that those at tables whose food was not yet served should feel free to jon the bride and groom on the dance floor. People rose from their seats.

Over at Annisquam, the Maid of Honor leaned toward two couples she had never met before. This wasn't her assigned table; she just happened to have alighted there. Propping herself up on her bony elbows, she hunched forward and opened her dark eyes wide. They were slightly bloodshot (lack of sleep, all that time spent in various airplanes, and now too much alcohol) as well as mildly asymmetrical, as if something inside her were skewed, too. "You know what they told us before we finally got on the plane? That the technical problem was repaired 'to the best of our knowledge.' To the best of our knowledge!" The two couples nodded awkwardly as she took a gulp of wine. "And we went ahead and got on the plane anyway!" She shook her head, and the bells of her dress trembled.

The skin below her eyes was puffy and splotched; she had cried unstoppably watching the bride and groom take their vows. Some guests on the bride's side said this was because Callie was the first best friend she had ever had. The two of them had grown up right next door to each other—until Callie's parents bought a bigger house in another part of town.

"I saw one of the repair guys step off the plane," she added seriously. "And do you know all that he was carrying? Duct tape!"

She was observed by the bridesmaids at Halibut Point as they discussed what they had purchased as wedding presents. "Nothing from her at all," they whispered, reveling in disgrace. As much as any of them liked her, it was always a relief to have someone else to be ashamed of.

"You'd think she of all people would at least get them a decent gift."

"Well, she has a full year from the wedding date, remember."

"You think they'll last that long? Just kidding."

They were eager to return to the captivating details—how even after Mack and Callie had gotten back together there had been something between him and the Maid of Honor, you could tell. None of them could have said why they found this story so fascinating, except that it had an element of tragedy as well as familiarity; they had all, at one point in their lives, been in the Maid of Honor's shoes.

"She'd been after him for years, apparently. Even when we were in college. Remember when she came to visit that time?"

"Right after that was when Mack dumped Callie."

"I thought Callie was the one who broke up with Mack."

"That was the second time, after college."

"Because of *her*."

"It's true. Callie told me."

"Then why would she make her Maid of Honor?"

"A consolation prize. You know how Callie is."

Indeed, that was just like her. She was the team captain who in gym class picked the unlikely athletes, the student who made a point of befriending the new kid or the underdog. Her latest plan had been for the Maid of Honor to hit it off with the Best Man. But in a shocking—if largely unnoticed—turn of events, the Best Man appeared to be smitten with a distant relative on the bride's side: a woman in her early forties who, though not in the bridal party per se, had been given a corsage and asked to read a passage from *The Little Prince.* Yet no one but the groom's mother had noticed the Best Man's affections, even though it had been perfectly obvious at brunch that morning, the way that he had angled for a seat next to the lovely light-eyed woman. Eileen, who still recalled him as a sweet teenage boy, had watched him ask the woman fawning questions, and had smiled to herself as he repeatedly offered to fetch her food from the buffet. No one else even seemed to be watching. It was as if, because they themselves could not see the appeal of a woman in her forties to a man in his thirties, the entire courtship must not be taking place. But Eileen herself had been loved, greatly loved, by a much younger man, and so she was able to see. After all, there was no good reason such a thing shouldn't happen, especially at a wedding, where there is little space of any other kind for a random middle-aged woman to inhabit.

Eileen watched as the Best Man, through with his announcement, fetched a drink for the light-eyed woman, while the woman pretended not to know exactly what was occurring between them. That's what you did in situations like this, where everyone was a bit compromised. You played your role and made sure the day was grand. You forgot about your own pleasures, and your own disasters. You smiled politely and held your breath—as big a gasp of air as possible, enough to last you, you hoped—and then you waited until it was over, when you could go back to being your full self.

But the cluster of bridesmaids was buzzing:

"He hasn't been at any job for more than a year."

"He keeps saying he's going to get an M.B.A., but he never gets the application in on time."

"I thought it was that he finished the application but missed the exam deadline."

"He applied on time but wasn't accepted. He doesn't have the grades. We all know he was a total partyer in college."

"So was Callie."

"But Callie excels at everything."

"It's just that he's unfocused. And then he was with that Internet startup, just when all the dot-coms started to go belly-up."

"I heard he got fired."

"Callie likes that kind of thing. Now she gets to be his savior."

Annie watched the Maid of Honor down more wine. It was possible Eileen was wrong about her after all. Maybe she wasn't such a good match for Mack. For one thing, she was an academic of some kind, and scholars were no fun as spouses; Annie knew because she herself was one (comparative philosophy) and understood what it meant to be mired in the petty imbroglios of university life. Plus, a woman endeared to serious, arcane study was sure to wear out her welcome with someone of Mack's aptitude for laziness.

And maybe Mack wasn't a good match for *her*. After all, if she could be this shaken by some sort of emergency landing, then how in the world could she ever put up with a man as carefree as Mack?

Annie had known Mack since his infancy, when he was a smiling, drooling baby with no clue of what life had to offer. Now here he was, twirling his bride with the bashful clumsiness of a man who rarely danced. Annie wondered what would happen with them. The furthest she could possibly see ahead for the two of them was the underbelly of a baby carriage stuffed with a mother's own toys: cell phone, water bottle, gym clothes, snacks. Even of this she wasn't quite sure. When you considered the realities of marriage, it really didn't matter how good or bad a match two people were.

Her own wedding day, nearly forty years ago, had been generally unpleasant. All morning long, huge storm clouds had loomed overhead, and even though they never broke, Annie had spent the entire reception worrying that they would, so that by the time the guests left she felt as if the whole world had been washed out in floods. Meanwhile, her husband had been cheerful as ever and seemed not to even notice how narrowly they had escaped disaster.

Surely it was better for Mack to marry someone like Callie, who would never worry about storm clouds, and who didn't quite know what it meant to not always enjoy life. Perhaps he shouldn't be with a person like the Maid of Honor, who, it was obvious, knew what it felt like to try hard and still not necessarily get what she wanted. Just look at her, too skinny, and in that bruise-colored dress, circles under her dark eyes. It probably was best for him to be with Callie.

For the time being, at least.

At Salt Island, already they were making a ruckus. The bride's side wondered what kind of people those were. Was it a fight, or was it just teasing? There were hoots and hollers, and the bride's father asked his wife, "What's going on over there?" But Helen, sparkling proudly in gold shantung, said, "Tom, honey, I think that's singing."

Then she gave a concerned glance toward Annisquam, where the Maid of Honor was pushing herself up out of her seat, taking noticeable pains to regain her balance. It seemed forever ago, thought Helen, that she had been a daily presence in their home, a little curly-haired girl, almost a second daughter. What a shame her parents couldn't be here. They had moved out to a condominium in Phoenix years ago, and Helen hadn't seen them in ages. The brother, too, now lived out west—and had apparently opted to take a last-minute Caribbean vacation rather than attend Callie's wedding. Well, better that her family wouldn't witness their daughter like this; she had always been such a good, good girl. Now she made her weaving way between other guests— excuse me, if you'll excuse me—navigating with effort, that tinny jangling sound warning of her arrival.

"The Girl with the Shaken Nerves," the Best Man joked as she walked past him, toward the dance floor. Then he dared to ask his new amour, "Shall we join her?"

Smiling, the light-eyed woman rose from her seat, and together they moved to where everyone was swaying and twirling and telling each other how they wished they had signed up for swing classes, or they had started to, or they had done so once, long ago. The two of them began to improvise, wondering lightly if any of the other guests were watching. While their union was an unorthodox delight it was also—though no one would have admitted it—just the sort of thing guests expect at weddings. After all, something had to happen. It was in the air. Everyone was waiting.

"They look good together, don't they," Eileen said to Annie, still seated at Magnolia.

"Definitely." But Annie was referring to the bride and groom, who were still dancing sloppily, energetically, against each other.

Calamity

A posse of bridesmaids appeared, and Callie ushered them around her, forgetting, it seemed, all about her new husband.

With his wife gone, Mack began to dance with the Maid of Honor, the bells on her dress whipping back and forth. Eileen watched her son, and watched the Maid of Honor, and watched her daughter-in-law, and watched the Best Man take his love interest by the hands. The two of them did a little inverse turn, hands over their heads, smiling when they managed not to get tangled, and the people watching them smiled, too.

Eileen could not take her eyes off these people she loved— even she had to admit, Callie, with her tall blondness and splendid curves. Only a few hours earlier that bright-eyed girl had been enthroned at a salon, a panoply of pins and spray in her hair. Now here she was, a married woman.

A gust of wind came through the tent, stirring up the linens and cooling the leftover mashed potatoes. Eileen watched as all around her women pulled their throws more tightly around their shoulders. She didn't believe in omens, and she had never taken weather personally. This was the ocean, after all, a harsher, more dangerous world, where seamen had braved all sorts of conditions in the name of blubber and shellfish and a nice fillet.

He wrapped her warm in his seaman's coat
Against the stinging blast;
He cut a rope from a broken spar,
And bound her to the mast.

Eileen inhaled deeply and tasted the fetid odor of the ocean. She was filled with a suddenly overwhelming question: what would happen?

Wedding at Rockport

. . .

"I remember the day when Callie was two and a half, maybe three years old," the bride's grandmother said in her crumbling voice. Now that her son-in-law had joined her daughter on the dance floor, there were just Eileen and Annie to hear her story.

"My daughter called me, out of breath. Her voice was shaking. I was so worried, my heart started pounding. Helen said, Something's happened with Callie, and my heart stopped. And you know what it was that had happened? It was that she was gorgeous."

As if to confirm this, all three of them looked out to the dance floor, where the bride was circled by bridesmaids, her cheeks full and flushed from dancing. Now that more people had finished their meals, the floor was filling up, physical motion warming the brisk evening.

Mack had managed to locate Callie among the pack of bridesmaids. Annie, tugging absently at her fruit earrings, saw him kiss her grandly and spin her around for a bit. He then leaned her back in a sloppy dip from which she gracefully recovered.

"Let's go," the Best Man called into the microphone, out of breath from his own exertions. "All of you, get out here and join us!"

"Come on, kiddo," Eileen said, nudging Annie, "let's you and me dance."

The music was suddenly turned up louder—a cue for everyone to join in. Annie found a spot on the dance floor and immediately began flapping her hands and wagging her broad hips. Eileen followed along and was swept up by her son, who seemed suddenly taller, lankier, as he took her by her bony hand.

"Just don't dip me," she told him. "Dip Annie instead."

The three of them danced in a little triangle, just like the old days, when Annie would visit them, balancing Mack on her knees as he bobbed along to music on the radio. Eileen looked around at the throng. What release, as if there were no such thing as troubles in life. As if life really could be—if we all just did this a bit more often—one big party. And yet surely they had all, everyone under the tent, contended with something. All around her, an array of shipwrecks.

Now Callie had arrived, and the four of them danced in a square for a bit, until she and Mack set off and left Eileen and Annie shimmying across from each other. In the center of the dance floor, Mack tossed Callie this way and that, and the DJ turned the spotlight onto her, and you could see her white underwear through her dress.

By the time the hour came for making toasts, the Maid of Honor was too drunk to say her speech. Not that anyone had expected otherwise. And yet there was a mild sense of disappointment in the air; they would have liked some kind of spectacle.

"It's a shame," Eileen said to Annie. "She can be pretty damn funny."

Of course, Annie thought. How could it have taken me so

long to notice? With her wiry limbs and inappropriate dress and all that implicit disapproval around her, the Maid of Honor must have reminded Eileen of the way she herself had been. A younger, darker—if less intrepid—Eileen.

They listened and laughed as the Best Man spoke, his toast full of little, loving jabs of just the sort that Eileen felt could do her son good.

The bridesmaids who didn't have boyfriends craned their necks to see better, wondering if the Best Man was truly single. The women who were mothers thought of what a good son he must be. Eileen wondered what would happen with him and his new love.

"And so," the Best Man concluded, "let's raise our glasses to two truly wonderful people who deserve not only each other but every other wonderful thing this life has to offer!"

There were cries of "Cheers!" and some spilt champagne, and over at Folly Cove an usher whistled. People laughed as the Best Man kissed the groom energetically on the lips, and when, as he embraced the bride, one of her bobby pins stabbed him in the cheek.

Amidst the hubbub, the Maid of Honor had managed to step up to the microphone. Like a ballerina en pointe, she stood in a commanding, if wobbly, way. Then she raised her glass and, with the purposeful clarity of a drunk, spoke:

"People," she said, looking straight out at the crowd.

"People—"

She formed her sentence carefully and very, very slowly, each word emerging just when it seemed she had forgotten what it was she meant to say.

"People have

drowned

so that this

day

could take

place."

She spoke with such conviction, with such finality, that, even though no one had even an inkling as to what she might mean, her words still seemed, to everyone, satisfyingly profound.

A contemplative hush came over the tent. Someone whispered something about haiku. The Maid of Honor breathed calmly as the Best Man, in his finest moment, swept up to the microphone.

"To all the *people*!" he cried, lifting his glass. "And to all of you!"

He then took the Maid of Honor by the elbow and led her away from the microphone. From the speakers came the waning sound of her dress, and throughout the tent people said another round of "Cheers!"—not so much to each other, this time, as to her.